# Wreck of the

# Gossamer

*The Puzzle Box Chronicles: Book 1*

# Wreck of the Gossamer

Shawn P. McCarthy

*The Puzzle Box Chronicles*
*Book 1*

*Dark Spark Press*

Book cover design by Teodora Chinde
Printed in the United States of America
First Printing, 2016
ISBN-13: 978-0996896702 (Dark Spark Press)

ISBN-10: 0996896708
**Dark Spark Press**
www.DarkSparkPress.com
Publisher.DarkSparkPress@gmail.com

For

**Awesome Dan**
&
**Amazing Kelly**

# Chapter 1

## *Half Life*

June 16, 1891

Cape Cod, Massachusetts

Amanda Malcolm steps back from a window and sits on the edge of her mattress. Quivering hands press tight against her forehead.

Behind her, cotton sheets lay rumpled atop an unmade bed — the remains of an empty white canvas upon which she had intended to paint the landscape of home. And love. And family.

But no such masterpiece exists.

They are not compatible painters, the pair who reside in this bedroom. They lack the shared vision for collaborative projects. The work is sadly left undone, canvas laid bare and the painters now at odds. They linger on in separate rooms of this farmhouse. Steps away yet miles apart.

One floor below the bedroom of this small Cape-style house she can hear her husband, Wayne, retreating to the kitchen. He slams pans across shelves and sorts through cluttered drawers in the kitchen. He seeks a misplaced bottle of whiskey. Amanda has not yet told him that she poured it out.

"Where is it?" Wayne shouts. His voice echoes through the floorboards. More clinks and scrapes come from below. "God damn it woman, if you hid it again, so help me …." Then the swear words come, low and vile and guttural. They stack one atop the other and cut like the teeth of a saw. His rants are worse even than what she remembers hearing as a child, from the dockworkers back in Boston.

There's a small thud, and Wayne's voice changes a bit. She knows he's done something. Banged a finger maybe. Or perhaps dropped something on his foot. He's so much harder to deal with in a rage of pain.

Bitsy, their gray and white cat, also senses his mood change. Amanda hears her whine and run up the stairs.

The thumping and clanking below come to a halt, and she hears the door to her spice cupboard open. Amanda knows he's found the vanilla extract again. Fine. Let him have that. The rage should subside when that small amount of alcohol kicks in. His beast will be cooled, maybe for the whole night. She stands again and looks out the dusty window. She feels tears drying against her face yet doesn't remember starting to cry. It all blends.

She'll be all right, she knows she will. She always is. She can be tough when she needs to be.

Amanda listens to the silence. Silly as it seems, she still cares about him. Wayne really isn't a bad man. He has a good heart. She's seen it in the way he treats the horses and the chickens. But both of their hearts have grown heavy with the pressures of the farm. And they simply aren't working well together. His drinking grows heavier each night.

Is she the cause? So hard to know. So many things that just ….

She runs her hands over the folds of her skirt, pressing fingers against fabric like magical flat irons. But the wrinkles remain, and her hands grow tired.

Staring past the window into the darkness, Amanda wishes she could see the ocean from here. She needs to see it. The salt waves, the reflections, the birds. All so close here on Cape Cod, yet kept from her sight. It's been far too long since she's gone down to the water. Far too long since she's felt small and humble, just standing at its edge.

Standing.

What if a man is never happy with the way a woman stands beside him? What if her support isn't what he needs and isn't properly cherished? How long is she expected to stay at that man's side, and he at hers?

Footsteps on the stairs. A low burp. She waits, futile fingers smoothing fabric yet again.

Thank God there are no children yet. That will make her decision easier. Yet, isn't it also part of the tension? Three years. No baby. The arrival of children is always the highly anticipated second act to a relationship. But there has been no second act for them. They are stuck in a lingering intermission.

"Come on out'a there, woman!" Wayne bellows from beyond the door. "I ain't going to hurt ya. Just want you to tell me … where's my god damn whiskey?"

She hears a snorking sound and pictures his too-big mouth trying to wrap around the tiny brown bottleneck of the vanilla, like a calf urgently nuzzling a teat.

"You've got your alcohol, Wayne! All right? Are you happy? You've got your drink now, so just leave me be!"

He exhales slowly, as if considering her plea. "No. No, I won't leave ya be, you damn shrew! You threw the whiskey out, didn't ya? I know ya did! I'm so fed up with ya! I'm fed up with all of it!"

Amanda doesn't turn toward the door. She just presses her forehead against the window glass. Trees in the yard are visible in the moonlight. Leaves silvery and restless. Tipped upwards. A storm is coming. She feels the tears this time as they start to form.

A farm that doesn't flourish can be a lonely place. The nearest neighbor is a quarter mile away. This place had seemed like the perfect escape for her, but the distance also brought isolation. Then distrust. Now she's terribly remote to everything else in the world. Unnoticed. Like the paint on the faded clapboards of the farmhouse.

Amanda, never a big woman in the first place, has become even thinner. Paler than ever. She is a falling raindrop, never quite reaching the ground.

"Go to bed, Wayne," she calls out. "Just … just go to bed."

He slaps at the door. "I can't. You're in my goddamn bed, woman!"

Then he laughs. Amanda knows that laugh. When she hears it, her back straightens and she brushes stray light-brown hairs from her forehead.

"Besides," he says, now with a playful lilt in his voice, "I don't want to go to bed yet."

"Now don't you start, Wayne. Not after the way you've been treating me. Don't you start that at all."

She hears him take a long suck on the bottle. It isn't just the vanilla making him disagreeable. He'd come home drunk too. The vanilla's just put him over the top.

If only it would put him to sleep.

A strong thud shakes the door. She blinks, then holds her temples.

"Open up, damn you! You're my wife, and don't you forget that. Don't you ever, *ever* forget that, 'Mrs. Malcolm.'" He sneers out the name like it's a label pasted on a piece of property.

He kicks the door twice more, laughing in self-satisfaction with each blow. The metal lift-latch bounces. Small screws in the slide bolt submit to the pressure and splinter out of the doorframe. Wayne stumbles in, mouth open, pants open too.

Drawing out the last swig from the bottle, he throws it hard against the wall.

"Well, looky you, all settled here in the bedroom waiting for me. Ain't that nice." He pushes his pants down farther. "And looky me, all ready for you too, huh?" She can see his state and realizes that he's not going to take no for an answer.

Amanda stares at his nakedness. Then she stares deep into his eyes. Then at the door.

"Come on, sweetie. Let's lay down. You don't even got to do nothin'. You just lie there, okay?" He slides his pants down past his knees. That's all she needs. Bolting toward him, she pushes him hard. Wayne stumbles backwards in a drunken gait. Lowered pants keep him from taking a balancing step, and he crashes down hard on his backside, howling when he lands on some of the vanilla bottle's broken glass.

Amanda leaps over and past him as he grabs at her feet. Catching her by an ankle, he slurs a string of threatening words, including a threat to kill her. She bends down and drives a knuckle into his wrist. She manages to stumble backward as he lets go and she grabs the broken doorframe. Then she lunges through it and on down the short staircase in three bounds. Grabbing her light summer shawl from a wall peg, she rushes out the front door.

The young woman runs into the blackness, biting her lip and puffing hard through her nose. She doesn't know where to go, or how long to stay away. The few people that she does know out here on Cape Cod were friends of Wayne's long before they became friends of hers. The true loneliness and isolation of her situation closes in like a dark, heavy blanket.

She's nearly across the yard when the rain starts.

When she reaches the edge of the dirt road at the far corner of their property, she simply stops and hangs her head. Drips fall from her small nose and fine chin. A waif who lacks the power to even run away.

Amanda stands for several minutes, refusing to do even so much as shiver.

This wasn't the life she chose. It wasn't even half of what she had hoped to build. And that's been the central question in her life for several weeks. Is half a life a reason to stay? Or is it half the reason she needs to just let it go?

The rain falls harder and colder. She walks back through her yard, temporarily defeated but determined not to return to the house. Instead, she heads toward their small barn.

Grunts from the milk cows greet her as she slides open the heavy door—just enough to squeeze inside. The familiar smells soothe her.

Amanda checks on each animal, mostly to give herself something to do. Jessie, her favorite cow, needs water. Another one needs a bit of hay. She walks through the barn, giving each cow and horse a little pat, settling them. Comforting herself in the process. Then she grabs a horse blanket and makes the precarious climb up into the hayloft. Despite her racing heart, despite her wet clothes, she tries to sleep, eventually losing herself in the soothing drone of chewing cows and raindrops on the tin roof.

Chapter 2

## *Gossamer*

Atlantic Ocean – North of Georges Bank

Wide circles carved over dark gray water. The wings of a gull stretch wide to catch a following wind. Mild updraft, warm moist air rising with it. Different temperatures. Different swirls. Perplexing eddies in the air. White feathers at the edge of darker wings slowly flare outward. Now there's a cooler breeze to ride. A sea bird feels every nuance in the wind.

Several miles to the east, a ten-year-old cargo ship chugs in a wide, slow loop. Its steam engines sound powerful and reliable, though its hull and scuppers are stained with scruffy grease and rust.

The ship's circular bearing is no accident. The skipper of the *Gossamer* has been paid to let his ship linger one extra day near the notorious fishing grounds above Georges Bank. One of the men on board, an oddly dressed man currently uncrating some strange-looking equipment, will use this time to conduct a series of technical experiments as the ship wanders in its slow circles.

Ocean smooth as glass. Clear skies. Warmth on the wind. That's the view seen by the sailors on this steamer. They're unable to feel what the gull feels much higher in the sky.

High above, that great black-backed gull, lingering hints of youth still speckling its neck, slowly banks to the left. Flapping hard and fighting the strengthening breeze, it heads toward the *Gossamer*, seeking brief purchase. Below the wind. Above the waves.

The glassy surface of the ocean slowly changes. Swells appear. The rising sea seems to come from two directions, pushed by competing sets of winds. The ocean assumes a different face now—that of marble, but not the polished white kind of surface. This marble is dull and black with twisted veins of ivory streaked across its surface, the white veins being ribbons of bubbles left behind when the competing wave patterns intersect, foaming forces that cancel each other's ambitions.

Wings held wide, the bird drops onto a stubby mast at the center of the steamship. The *Gossamer* is a wide, twin-engine ocean-going steamer. Its short masts are little more than a backup plan, employed only if both engines fail—an unlikely occurrence on a well-built vessel. Like most ships plying the Atlantic in the 1890s, the *Gossamer* has two large paddlewheels—port and starboard sides. Through a series of shafts and levers, either of the engines could be called upon, if needed, to run one or both of the side-wheels.

The men on the deck were carefree just minutes before. Now they seem agitated by the sudden weather change. Crates holding strange equipment need to be resealed. Deck gear must be stowed.

There's apprehension in the sailors' voices. Hints of dissension in their ranks. Some say they should turn south.

Others say west. But they stick with the captain's choice. His course sends them east by southeast as the main part of the storm bears down from the northeast. There's a fair chance they can throttle up the engines and scoot around it.

Below the perched gull, three men stand near the largest of the crates. One hastily plucks two intricate, highly polished wooden boxes off its top, hauling them away in a sack.

"Where ya going with those?" another man calls out.

"Below! Going to stow 'em!"

"Well, you be careful with those, ya hear? That's my future in there!"

Victor Marius, holding the sack, looks back and nods. Victor is the man with the strange clothes and the strange crates. He is the man who hired the *Gossamer* to spend an extra day traveling in circles, roughly 100 miles off the coast of Massachusetts.

This man Victor, the other men on the ship have realized, is an enigma. They've learned that he has the sea in his blood. His father, Eli, was a sailor. So was his grandfather. Victor told them when he was a child, he was one of the dozens of dirty-faced kids who skittered around the greasy docks lining Boston Harbor. In his youth perhaps half the visiting ships were still powered by sail. Victor loved the celebrated look and lines of the old sailing ships. Yet, even as a boy, he knew their days were numbered. The world already was changing to steam.

Victor's love for all things new and mechanical drew him to the increasingly reliable steamships, and whenever a new steamer arrived in the city, he'd race out to see it. With a wondrous smile he'd watch it hiss and clank its way to the piers. Then he'd stand nearby as it tied off, tossing questions to any crewmember who would listen to him.

What's the length? Beam? Displacement? Horsepower? Cargo? He gathered facts like stolen taffy, tucked away for later consumption and enjoyment.

But even with the sea in his blood, Victor seems more like a contraption-building industrialist than a sailor. In Boston he had originally studied to be a marine architect, then switched to mechanical engineering at the twenty-five-year-old Massachusetts Institute of Technology. After two years, feeling increasingly unfocused and unsure of himself, he found his true calling. His interest lay not on the water, nor in the hiss of ever-larger steam machines. He tied his future to the blossoming domain of electricity, the fastest-growing technology of all.

Even though fledgling electric motors had been invented decades before, Victor could count on one hand the number of times people had talked about electricity when he was a boy—unless those people were attempting to describe the lightning in the sky or the sparks that danced across wool sweaters on winter evenings. Static electricity. No other explanation given, or needed, or even comprehended. It remained a crackling mystery.

But then the electric lightbulb appeared. People took notice. Soon electricity became the topic of conversation everywhere. Every community wanted this new power. And Victor was becoming an expert in the mysterious craft.

But, even as Victor set sail on the *Gossamer* that summer day, less than one percent of homes and businesses across

America's forty-four states were wired for electricity. Yet for all its growth potential, it's not electricity that brings Victor to the deck of the *Gossamer*. It's something beyond even that. His tests are aimed at something so new, different, and wonderful that he himself is still trying to understand it.

The storm forces him to hastily pack up his equipment, but until then he has busied himself investigating an exotic new concept called *radio*. He is the only man on the *Gossamer*, and one of only a handful of people in the world, who understands even a small portion of this strange and wondrous phenomenon.

He'd been looking forward to this set of tests for weeks. And now they must wait. After stowing the equipment, he heads below to stow the sack containing two beautifully polished wooden boxes.

*Yes*, he thinks, *a very interesting future indeed* in those boxes.

Victor returns to the rolling deck. He finds it deserted.

Clanking sounds come from a hatch. A fellow sailor sticks his head up and yells, "Everything safe? Pack up all your gear?"

"Yes, Johnny, I sure did."

Suspicion in the sailor's eyes.

"And yes," he continues, "both of our puzzle boxes are safe too. Tucked in nice and neat. We're going to have to wait until tomorrow to finish them."

Johnny C. nods, then offers a little smirk.

"But you already knew that, didn't you?" Victor laughs. "You just went to check them, didn't ya? That's why you were below just now."

"Aye. That I did, lad," Johnny C. admits. "Like I said. That's my future in there. My valuable cargo. Hate to let it out of my sight, especially since you know now what I have in there. Stupid of me to tell so much, I reckon."

"Well, what the hell?" Victor shrugs. "Sometimes you have to tell someone. Right? And you have to be able to trust your shipmates."

Johnny C. snorts. "You haven't spent much time on ships, have you? Desperate men sign on as sailors, lad. Not the most trustworthy lot."

He nods toward the crates. "So, you've packed everything else back up too? All your experiments and such? Too bad you have to wait."

The ship rocks. Victor reaches for the edge of the wheelhouse to steady himself, then points to the sky. "I'd say I definitely have to wait. Look at that!"

A dark cloud mass has assembled and piled higher, now reaching hundreds of feet into the air. Its appearance is abrupt and troubling.

"Looks like a damn nor'easter forming up," Johnny C. shouts. "Storm like that could push us sideways all the way back to Boston!"

Leaning against the wind, Victor pulls a hammer out of his belt as he walks back to his crates and pounds a few extra nails into the lids. He notices some hinged rings recessed in the deck, so he finds a couple ropes to drape over the boxes, then attaches them to the rings.

Johnny pops up a bit higher from the hatch and rests his arms on the deck. "What the hell is all that stuff in them crates anyway?"

Victor tugs and tests until he's satisfied with the tie-down. "Jesus, not now Johnny. I'd have to find a pencil and paper and I'd need to draw the whole thing out in order to explain it to you. How about if I tell you about it tomorrow when we unpack again?"

Affronted, Johnny shrugs. "All right. Fine, never mind."

But Victor can see the thoughts ticking in Johnny C.'s head. He's managed to latch onto the concept, however vague. Pointing west, Johnny shouts, "You did say you wanted to send a message back to land. Right? Can you really do that? From way out here? How can you do that without a telegraph line? Sounds like voodoo to me."

Victor laughs. "Yeah, well, maybe it is voodoo. But that's why I'm here. I want to see if the idea is real, or if it's just a crazy dream."

Johnny just shakes his head, then they quickly climb below.

# Chapter 3

## *The Banging of the Gate*

Amanda Malcolm awakens with a start, as the lilting bleat of a goat fills her head.

She keeps her eyes shut. Not yet willing to concede that it's morning. Sounds and smells swirl around her.

Fresh hay.

The pungent presence of farm animals. Clucks from chickens.

Behind all, there lingers the vaguest scent of the blue morning glories that grow just outside the barn. She doesn't need to open her eyes to remember that the barn was where she slept. She also remembers why.

Sitting up slowly, she looks down from the loft, trying to blink herself awake. Her gaze moves past the door and toward the warm dirt strip that serves as a path between house and barn. Paths go two ways, right? A man and a woman can stay at either end of a path, or they can meet in the middle. She and Wayne need to find the right compromise to get back what's missing from their once cherished life. She misses that connection. Perhaps he misses it too.

A cow softly groans as Amanda descends the ladder. Chickens rush over to mill about her feet.

Stroking Jessie's fur. Mucking out the horse stall. She'll feed the animals too, before taking the short walk up to the house.

She spreads corn for the Rhode Island Reds. Yellow dots skitter across the dirt floor. She laughs as the chickens bob their absurd heads. Amanda grabs and tosses another handful of kernels, just to enjoy the show.

She finds herself prolonging her chores by talking softly to each animal. Simple yet soothing comments.

"There you go. My, aren't you hungry? Don't eat it all at once, silly! You're looking shiny and healthy today."

And then she sees him, leaning against the barn door. Watching her.

Amanda turns away, scattering more feed. "Surprised you're up," she declares after several moments. "Your head must hurt." She nervously continues the scattering motion, even though there are but a few kernels left in her hand.

Wayne sighs and looks down, surprisingly contrite.

"Okay, so ... I guess you know I'm sorry about all that. It's just ... well ... you know how I get."

Amanda nods, gritting her teeth. "Since you know it too, why do you do it?"

"Look, don't lecture me, woman. I said I was sorry, didn't I?"

She bites her lip and walks over to lift more straw into the horse stall—even though there's already plenty there.

Wayne mutters something mildly acquiescent, waits for a few seconds, then walks away. The conversation ends before another argument evolves. These days that's what passes for an uneasy peace between them.

Amanda and Wayne avoid each other for the rest of the morning and most of the afternoon. She works in the barn and in her garden. He works in the fields. Later in the day when she comes inside to start dinner, she finds him sleeping at the kitchen table.

Clanking pots bring him awake.

"Chickens need more feed," he mumbles. "I'll take the wagon."

Avoiding eye contact, he walks to the counter and struggles to pull open a jammed kitchen drawer. Its wood swollen by the humid June weather.

"The chickens are fine, Wayne. There's more than half a sack out there. That's enough to see us 'til Saturday."

"I ain't going to town on Saturday," he lies. "Least not until late in the day. So I'm getting some damn feed today, understand?"

"What about dinner?"

"Keep it warm." He uses a butter knife to pry open the drawer, chipping some of the already peeling paint around its edge. He takes out a pair of work gloves and a handkerchief.

Amanda closes her eyes as he leaves.


Once dinner is cooked, she waits for a while. Then she eats it out on the porch by herself. It's tender mutton and noodles with fresh yellow beans. In better times she and Wayne would often eat on the porch together, laughing, talking, and watching the sunset.

The smell of honeysuckle drifts in from the fields as she takes her last bite. Bushes cast ever-longer shadows toward the house. She places the plate on the deck beside her. Bitsy appears and licks it clean.

A musty but sweet scent also lingers. It comes from a small ditch that runs along the south side of their property. Wild lilies grow there, flared orange blossoms still visible in the moonlight.

*Gutter flowers.* That's what her grandfather called them. He gave her the same name—but as a term of endearment.

"Those bright lilies don't care where they grow," the old man said. "They seem to especially like soggy ditches. A flower like that can draw beauty out of any old, rotten place. A gutter flower makes its gutter a better place just by being there." Then he'd whisper in her ear. "Try to bloom where you're planted, girl. If you can. This is a damn gutter where this family is living, but the right flower can make it a better place. And be damn proud of your beauty as you grow."

But Amanda didn't take Grandpa's words to heart. She didn't stay where she was planted. She left the gutters of Boston, and she came out here to the Cape. Here to join Wayne.

One other thing she knows about those wild orange lilies is if you pick them, the bloom withers in just a couple hours. Unlike roses or tulips, a wild lily isn't happy when it's picked. A wild lily that's removed from its gutter often just wilts and dies.


Wayne doesn't return until after eleven that night. Amanda has left the house and climbed back up to her barn loft. Wayne settles onto the porch. She hears the clink of a bottle touching a drinking glass. He calls to her, and she answers only that she's in the barn.

The bottle pours again. Wayne yells to her every fifteen minutes or so using a string of comments that don't really amount to anything other than anger and resentment.

He shouts comments like, "Ya ain't going to live in that barn forever, woman!" and "Well, fine then, you just go on and stay in there, you hear me? What the hell do I care?"

There are long pauses between every shout. In between, she wonders if he's fallen asleep. But then more curses and comments spill forth.

"Yeah?" he slurs. "Well, what the hell's the matter with ya anyway? Damned if I know. Damned if anyone can figure out the likes of you."

A sudden thud brings Amanda upright. At first, she thinks he may have fallen off the porch. Then she realizes it's just his empty bottle, tossed out into the yard.

"Don't know what the hell I saw in ya in the first place. I really don't," he bellows. "Shoulda seen you was crazy! Shoulda seen that first thing, I reckon. But I didn't. I was some kind of fool."

On it goes, his words growing weaker and more difficult to understand. Mumbles in the dark.

Amanda barely sleeps, rising finally at three o'clock in the morning. As she slips out of the barn, she can see him still sitting in the porch chair, head slumped forward and arms hanging down at his sides like vines from a withering tree.

The night before she had promised herself that she'd see the ocean. She'll finally do that. She can walk there if she wants. No need even to saddle the horse. Once she reaches the water, she'll remove her shoes and stockings, hold her dress up, and run through the surf.

Amanda races across the front lawn with an anxious heart. Away from the barn. Away from the farmhouse. The front gate bangs as she leaves, and she hurries eastward toward the vaguest hint of morning sunlight.

# Chapter 4

## *Wind & Wave*

Ship turning, bobbing, unable to sustain its compass heading.

Johnny C. climbs out of his hatch, battens it tight, then sprints for the rear one. That opening leads to the engine room two decks below.

Returning to the crew quarters, Victor discovers that the bag with the two puzzle boxes has slid out from under his bunk. There's no easy way to wedge it in place, so he finds a narrow slot between the bunk and the wall and places the bag there, wedging a towel next to the bed support to hold the boxes in place. Thinking for a moment, he takes his own box back out then slowly breaks it apart, nimbly working its intricate puzzle, peeling back the multiple levels. He remembers what Johnny C. said—that a sailor can store important valuables inside. Working quickly, he picks up various items that mean something to him and places them inside the box, slowly reassembling it as he goes. He grabs things from a shelf near his bunk. Other items come from his footlocker. He also pulls out some clothes, rummaging through the pockets, finding more things to slide into in the narrow top layers of the box. With all the items inside and the puzzle fully reassembled, he slides it back in place beneath the bunk, wedging the towel back into its space.

Standing, Victor looks down the middle of the small cabin. Eight bunks line the walls. The upper one, at the far end, belongs to a sailor who enjoys dropping a fishing line over the side when they are in the shallows. Victor saw the man catch two small cod the previous evening. That sailor also keeps a sawed-off double-barrel shotgun on the wall above his bunk. He only takes it down when he's fishing, keeping it handy in case he snags a dog shark instead of a cod.

"Them little sharks, boy, they go nuts when hooked," he explained to Victor. "They go weaving back and forth under the boat, maybe even get themselves into a paddlewheel. They make a big mess of things if you let them. This here shotgun puts a right quick end to that nonsense, let me tell ya."

As the boat heaves, Victor staggers over to make sure the gun is securely fastened. It would be foolish to allow it to shake loose, falling and maybe discharging. Satisfied that it's secure, he dogs down the compartment's single ten-inch porthole, then heads back up to the deck.

The clouds look snarling and angry. Wispy streaks of rain hang down—gray, wet dishrags floating from the sky. The rain seems to fly toward them alarmingly fast, pushed sideways at the same time. The swells, which had been coming from opposite directions just moments ago, now seem to join together. The water in front of the *Gossamer* piles up like a hill, then churns and folds, producing a tall washboard of mini-whitecaps. The liquid mountain reminds Victor of a beer glass being filled too quickly, its foam head rising and spilling over the top.

Why hadn't they seen this coming? Why hadn't they been more careful? Victor curses to himself as he stumbles along the pitching deck. This storm lurked just a few hours away, and yet they never knew it was there. So sudden. So perilous.

Who could have prevented this? Maybe Victor himself. That's why his work is so important. He reminds himself of that as he struggles out of the compartment. Radio, if he and others are able to perfect it, could be immensely valuable to ships at sea. Messages could be relayed. Notices of storms, enemy ships, icebergs, all of that, could be shared. Evasive action could be taken. Lives could be saved.

Victor finds the other hatch and descends into the warmth of the engine room. He reaches the edge of boiler #1 just as new swells start to tilt the ship. Until that moment, the *Gossamer* had mostly bobbed up and down, with an occasional fishtail motion. But this time the ship leans nearly twelve degrees before slowly moving back to center. Not terrible. But troubling.

The action is followed by a steep drop. Victor absentmindedly grasps the boiler to steady himself. He hears a slight hiss followed by searing pain in his hand. Swearing, he jerks his hand away, instinctively sticking all his burned fingers into his mouth.

The pain must be ignored. He instead analyzes the sailors' worried faces and quickly realizes something is not right. Swells usually don't build this quickly. In most storms the sea typically produces eight-foot swells, which slowly build to twelve-foot swells, then sixteen-foot and so on. It typically takes a half hour or so for each increase of two feet in height.

Feeling swells of this magnitude on the very leading edge of the storm makes everyone in the engine room nervous. They look at each other, but say nothing. Has the worst of the storm come right at its start? Or is this just a taste of its power, with the worst yet to come?

# Chapter 5

## *Shack*

The gate, closing with a loud clank, awakens Wayne from his troubled sleep. An aggravated urgency compels him to follow, but his mind is hazy and his direction uncertain. Amanda hears him stumbling, bull-like, off the porch. A string of curses follow as he crashes into the flowerbeds below.

Wayne is in no shape to run, and it wouldn't matter if he could. With her dress hiked above her knees, Amanda is pretty fast. Only a few years earlier, she was outrunning most of the boys in her North Boston neighborhood. Kids would chase each other and throw apples, but she was wily enough that no one ever hit her.

She jogs in a steady gait. In twenty minutes she's close enough to the sea that she picks up the pungent smell of low tide. But there's no direct path from her house to the ocean. Instead, she must follow the road to the east. Eventually she'll pick up a winding trail that leads through the marshes.

As she slows to a walk, she looks at the sky and wonders if this trip should serve as the more formal escape she's long contemplated. Perhaps she should just run to a neighbor's house and ask for asylum.

Maybe Widow Ryan? Now there's a woman who would understand her plight. Even though Amanda doesn't know her well, she does know that Widow Ryan would take her in immediately and probably make her a cup of tea. They likely would talk and talk for hours. She's already heard stories from the old woman about the lot of a farmer's wife. She knows how lonely that life can be, and she's always helpful to others—with better advice than most other women Amanda had met.

Twice she hears wagons on the road and ducks into the tall grass. If no one sees her, she'll have no explaining to do.

Wagons pass. She walks on. More hints of light from the east. Then something touches and surprises her. Raindrops on her face. Thunder in the distance.

With salt flats all around her, there's no decent place to hide. Determined, she grasps her dress collar tightly and bows her head. In ten minutes she's nearly across the flats and heading toward high banks near the water's edge. There she sees a few small fishing shanties sitting precariously on the dunes. She's been here before. If it was daytime, the shanties would look bright and colorful with shades of yellow and green. But in the dim early morning, they look muted and gray.

A low rumble warns that the thunder is coming closer. If she needs shelter, this is the only place to find it. Best to take it now. It occurs to Amanda that barn-like structures have been good sanctuary for her during the past few days.

By the time she reaches the door of the closest shanty, the rain is in full force, slipping in cool rivulets down her neck and between her breasts. Her dress seems like flypaper sticking to her skin.

Inside she stumbles over a pile of fishing nets. She also sees faded red and white buoys, used to mark lobster pots when they are placed out in the shallows. She moves to the back of the room and settles down behind a pile of raincoats and tarps. She pulls one of the tarps over her, both to stay warm and to hide, in case anyone else ventures into the shack.

Then she rests. After a few minutes she pulls up a second tarp, then a third, to help stay the chill caused by her wet clothes. The rain beats a steady drone, and soon she falls asleep, making a quiet promise to herself to awaken just before the full sunrise.

# Chapter 6

## *Hanging On*

The waves are coming from different angles too. The age and the side-wheel design of the *Gossamer* actually helps its stability. Newer propeller-driven steamers have their sterns built out in an oddly flat way. It makes the rear end stronger against the increased torque of the props. But it also makes those ships extra vulnerable in bad weather.

The *Gossamer* has a rounded transom with a slight inward taper. As the leading edge of the storm passes, they somehow end up with a following sea. Their rounded stern divides the breaking waves instead of taking them like a slap. It also reduces the chance that the ship will be flipped end over end.

Being able to absorb a following sea is good news for the ship and its sailors. Victor remembers these design lessons from his short stay in marine architecture classes. Thus he also knows that the bad thing about a heavily rounded stern is that it can increase your chance of broaching, or being knocked over on one side. In a metal-hulled craft like this one, if you broach and don't quickly recover, you may not recover at all. The sea can twist a ship as it tilts—just enough to spring a hatch or a porthole. An iron boat like this one is strong, but once flooded, it could go down terribly fast. A wooden ship, on the other hand, might be weaker against the waves, but at least it's more buoyant. A wooden ship can be half full of water and it might still right itself. Riding low, a good wooden ship might be able to keep floating for a day or two, giving other ships time to find it. The crew might even have enough time to bail her out.

Victor can't help but think about this boat taking on just enough water to groan its last, spiraling toward the bottom like a stone. Those who wait for them at home will end up waiting forever.

He finds some grease to rub into his injured hand. It soothes the burn slightly. Farley the engineer tries to cool the boilers a bit, barking orders in short bursts. The trick, in a storm, is to keep the engines running. The captain needs enough power to steer the ship and avoid taking the waves broadside. But you don't want the boilers super-heated to the point that they'll crack if seawater ends up flooding the compartment. It's a delicate dance, and the crew performs it well, listening to the engineer's orders and reacting, and hearing occasional commands from the captain, barked through a metal tube that runs to the bridge.

Small shovels of coal. Tiny adjustments to the pressure valves. *Close that fire door sailor! Open that vent.* Standing in ankle-deep water, they try to keep the machine in tune with its rapidly changing environment.

The side wheels on the *Gossamer* spin independently. Besides using the rudder, the captain can also speed one paddle and slow the other, quickly pivoting the ship on a dime if needed. But the ship will move like that only if the wheels can bite. In a steep wave, the paddlewheel on one side or the other may pull out of the water for a few moments, causing the ship to lumber unpredictably to port or starboard.

Farley is well liked for his skills, if not his demeanor. "Grab the loose gear!" the chief shouts to Victor as he grabs more grease from the bucket. Victor knows he'd better comply. If he's not able to help the crew, then he's dead weight in this emergency. Victor looks around. He sees boots, some loose tools, coal buckets, and more lying near the edges of the engine room. As the ship lumbers, these items start to roll around in the water that has collected on the boiler-room floor. He gathers everything he can see, hoping to stow them in lockers at the back of the compartment.

"No! Ya blooming ass, don't worry about that shit right now. Topside! Batten the things on the deck first. If it looks valuable, toss it down the hatches. Anything looks like it's worth less than five dollars, throw the damn things overboard, and be quick!"

Victor stumbles up two sets of ladders. Forcing the hatch open, he again steps out onto the open deck. Green water rushes into his face. Blinking and coughing, he falls to his knees. He finds it difficult to slam the hatch shut this time, but finally secures it. The deck is awash with foam and fear. Behind him he hears someone banging shut another hatch. The sound worries him. Can these be opened again? Is he trapped out here? He shakes off the dread and tries to work.

He spots another sailor farther up the deck, unrecognizable in a black slicker. The man shouts to him and points toward some ropes that wiggle atop the brine. The message is clear: *Tie yourself off if you're planning to walk topside. If you don't, you might be washed overboard, and sure as hell no one is going to jump in after you.*

Victor loops the rope around his waist and ties a good square knot. Staring at it for a moment, he ties another for insurance. *If you can't tie good knots, tie several.* That's what his father, Eli, told him.

The rain stings and penetrates deep. His hands are shaking. He can feel the spar deck teetering not just port to starboard but around its center point too. The whole ship seems like a slowly spinning dinner platter.

Working with the other sailor, he does manage to clear the deck, finding many small and potentially dangerous objects skimming along the boards. Pieces of scrap wood. Bottles. Hats and shirts. He throws most of them over the rail. A clear deck is imperative. When a wave breaks over the bow of any ship, it washes along the deck and out the scuppers. It's usually a self-clearing system. But garbage can be washed into the scuppers too, blocking them. With no exit, the excess water can build up on the deck. A ship can suddenly gain several thousand pounds, making it top-heavy and much more likely to roll.

Victor is surprised. A tightly run ship would never allow loose items like these to accumulate on the deck. But here they are. He finally makes his way to one of the scuppers and pulls out what looks like a dead seagull. He looks up at the empty mast and then tosses the body overboard.

Victor has been on other voyages where the captain of those ships walked around at all hours, checking every tiny thing, lecturing the sailors, looking for problems at every turn—being total bastards but keeping everyone safe.

He suddenly realizes that he's seen the captain of the *Gossamer* only once on this entire trip, for about five minutes.

When he finishes clearing, Victor pulls off his hat and stuffs it into a vent pipe over the galley stove, sealing that small hole as best he can. Just then the tip of a large wave breaks over the stern, sending a thigh-high river of cold salt water rushing down the deck, knocking Victor onto his back. He slides a few feet as water blasts up his nose. The *Gossamer* immediately starts to climb the next swell, causing Victor to immediately slide the other way, down half the length of the deck, on his back, headfirst. He panics at the thought of slamming into something and breaking his neck, but suddenly his safety rope stops him with a violent jerk—just short of the taffrail. He tries to grasp the rail but can't quite reach it.

Instead he grasps the safety line and pulls, trying to take up the slack. Just then the ship reaches the top of the swell. Uphill immediately changes to downhill. The bow pitches into a new valley of water at such a steep angle that Victor can't stand up. Instead, he slides forward again, this time on his belly. He holds his hands in front of him, feeling like he's flying.

Victor has a sudden epiphany. Sailing is for crazy men. Only the certifiably insane should be out here in the middle of the ocean.

In some way that thought makes him feel better about his situation. He's never been a sailor. He's just a visitor here. That means this isn't really his storm. It's not his ship that's in peril. Others may die at sea. But not him. Not today. He feels like he's observing this danger from afar, waiting for the real sailors to suffer the consequences for their terrible mistake.

He grabs at the corner of the elevated wheelhouse as he slides past, fingers finding minimal purchase in a small vent. His body swings like a pendulum, crashing into the bulkhead, but he holds fast. Glancing up, he sees the ship's first mate standing inside, staring at him through the window. He barely hears the first mate shout, "Hang on!" as he stares, wide-eyed, toward the bow. Victor realizes that another wave must be coming. Hugging the wall, foot braced against a davit, he closes his eyes and feels the deck shake as the next wave crashes over, cold white foam hammering all around him. He feels the whole ship slip sideways and bump like a wild toboggan ride, falling into sea foam that seems to offer no support at all. The rushing sea leaves Victor cold, buried, and sore.

Foam like that is not good. He may not be real a sailor, but Victor's been on the sea enough to know the waves are breaking hard now. The swells have reached such a height that they're cresting over on themselves.

When a ship is facing only big swells, it can ride up and down and fight to stay upright. But when swells change into huge breaking waves, the angle of those "mountains of water" changes too. Things get too steep. Instead of just lifting, the water starts slapping. When that happens, it's no longer a matter of staying afloat. It's a matter of staying alive.

# Chapter 7

## *Light, Elusive*

After the steep, foam-filled wave passes over the deck of the *Gossamer*, the first mate rushes to the wheelhouse door, tugging at the locks. He reaches out into the storm, grasps Victor's safety rope, and pulls him inside.

"Are you crazy?" he yells as he re-bolts the hatch. "What are you doing out there? You think that damn rope is going to hold you when we take the next big one?"

"I know! I know!" Victor shouts. "I was just helping clear off the deck. I didn't think it would get this bad. Hell, it didn't look this bad even five minutes ago."

They both look toward the front of the wheelhouse. The captain has taken the wheel, white knuckles gripping it as he threads the bow carefully into each wave. "Aye," the first mate mutters, "reckon none of us thought it would get this bad."

"Anything I can do?" Just as Victor asks the question the *Gossamer* takes a wave directly broadside. Both of them are thrown toward the starboard side, crashing against the paneling. Victor has a fleeting image of his body swinging like a rug beater against the side of a stiff carpet. But the image is abruptly erased as he bangs his head. The captain manages to remain upright, hanging from the wheel and growling as he braces a foot against the wall. He fights to right the ship. Victor shakes the dazed feeling from his head and then pulls himself up using the large gimbaled brass compass. As he rises, he sees that the top face of the compass assembly has pivoted nearly out of sight. The compass is still facing up. It's the ship that has tilted.

Slowly, impossibly slowly, the *Gossamer* manages to right itself, and the compass follows suit between Victor's trembling hands.

"Aye, there's a good girl," the captain growls at the ship. "You stay upright now, ya hear?"

A strange thumping sound starts to shake the freighter. They all realize it's coming from the port-side paddlewheel. The impact, which rolled them temporarily toward starboard, must have bent the housing, pressing the metal sheathing against the spinning port wheel. Not good news, but thank God the wheel can still turn.

"Get below," the captain shouts to Victor and the other man. "If the engine room can't use your help, climb down to the damn bilge and see if anything's leaking. And if they can't use your help there, just get to your bunks and lay low. Stay the hell out of the way."

Victor nods, burned hand holding his bruised head as he trips down the short ladder into the second-level companionway. Spying two inches of water on the floor, he shouts up to the captain. The only reply is a grunt.

Water can always find a way in. Seal the ship tight, and the ocean still seems to find the very pores of the hull. The harder the waves slap, the more the sea forces its way in, rattling hatches and popping caulking from the deck boards. Two inches of water on the middeck might be nothing, or it might be everything. Victor will know more when he gets a bit lower in the ship.

He goes down, finds no real problem on the lower deck. Comes back up again, running toward the stern. One of the quirks in the design of the *Gossamer* is that the crew can't walk the whole length of the ship on its lowest decks. There are watertight bulkheads between three sections, and they were built with no hatches. This keeps the sailors constantly climbing up and down as they move about the ship.

Back down again into the engine room, he finds the water is indeed deeper—now nearly a foot. Two sailors are bailing, pushing and pulling on the long handle of a double hand pump. This is a surprise because pumping of this magnitude isn't usually done by hand. There is supposed to be a long belt running from the portside engine to a flywheel on a central pump station. Victor sees the big belt. It's frayed and split, attached to nothing and lying in the water. His suspicion about how shipshape the *Gossamer* really is has just been confirmed.

Despite his injuries, Victor steps in to give one of the men a break. The three rotate in and out of the hand-pump station for the next twenty minutes. But they're slowly losing the battle. Glances are exchanged all around. When you're losing ground to a leak, everyone on board knows it, but no one wants to say it aloud.

The talk in the engine room is that the water is finding its way in somewhere near the damaged portside wheel.

"We need to get out of here!" Johnny C. finally declares. "The boiler will blow once the water reaches it."

"Belay that!" Farley screams back "We're not going to abandon the engine room. If we let that boiler tank blow, she'll rip the sides out and we're dead men for sure." He looks them all in the eyes. "Pump harder, lads. For God's sake, pump like your lives depend on it, because they sure as hell do."

The men stay at their stations, working faster, sweating so much they seem to be adding water to the oily brine at their feet. Through the extra effort they seem to win the battle for a while. But exhaustion sets in. They slow. Others appear to take their places. But with each relentless ocean wave, more saltwater seems to ooze into their space.

During the chaos one of the smaller sailors has climbed down and squirmed into the crawlspace near the damaged paddlewheel. He stays low, slipping beneath the huge moving shaft, following the space toward the spot where the fat axle of the side wheel penetrates the hull. There's water in here, but he manages to keep his head and a small lantern above the cold puddles. The sailor calls out when he finds two small leaks. The other men toss things from behind him, offering rags and wax, coal tar and shovels. The sailor takes everything that's handed to him, packing what he can into the leaks. He demands more, and they throw him whatever they can find: shirts, ropes, even a newspaper. The cramped sailor then covers the packing with grease and more wax. His work helps stem the flow.

"I don't think that was the main source of the leak!" he shouts as he claws his way out of the slot. "There's no way all this water's coming from just those small holes."

The crewmen start looking elsewhere. On his next break from manning the pump, Victor joins a sailor he's never met.

The man is seeking someone to come with him to the lowest point of the ship, into the tiniest of crawlspaces down near the keel. Victor shudders. He doesn't like small spaces, but he agrees to help.

They descend into the middle section where there is a deck hatch into the lowest bilge area. The other sailor kicks and scratches until he locates a flush-mount handle. Yanking open the heavy wooden door, he drops into a tight space, then edges forward in a squat. He has to hold his head high to keep it out of the neck-high water. Victor takes a deep, nervous breath and drops in behind him, gasping as the cold brine sends sharp prickles all over his body. He holds a lantern high, and the two of them waddle down the V-shaped slot for maybe eighteen feet, until they are actually under the main crawl that runs along the side of the paddlewheel. There, they see what they didn't want to see. On the inside of the hull, beside the very bottom of the portside wheel, there's a large dent in the hull. A pair of overlapping metal panels have split. Their rivets have popped. The leak is not unstoppable, but the amount of water spilling in is definitely more than what the pump men could ever hope to handle.

Victor learns that the other man, whose name is George, is the ship's resident expert at plugging leaks. He sends Victor back up the ladder, on a mission to grab several things that can be used to slow the influx. For the first time, Victor feels hopeful. Maybe things will get better now, if they can just hang on.

The ship lists at least ten degrees by the time he returns with a series of wooden wedges, plus some cork, rags, rubber, and wax. And he finds that the water in the slot is now nose deep. Nervously he squats and waddles his way toward the damaged plates. George the leak expert quickly takes the items from him. He holds his breath, dives, and desperately fills the split, determined to stop the flow. Victor takes a turn too. They dive and dive again, hands becoming numb as they work just three feet below the waterline.

Victor climbs back out, seeking even more rope and rubber. He sees other men run toward the stern. When he thinks about the amount of water he's already seen in the engine room, plus what he's just seen near the keel, plus what's now spilling down the ladders, he feels a terrible sense of dread. But they're patching the holes, aren't they? And pumping too. Maybe that will help. He has to keep trying.

The hope is short-lived. He hears shouts and notes of panic in distant voices. Then he feels a slow, steady list. The ship tips an additional fifteen degrees toward the port side, and the engine starts to falter. Far above him he hears someone on the deck struggling with the lifeboat davits. Suddenly a hand thrusts up through the open hatch at Victor's feet. Grasping that hand, Victor pulls George up from the keel's bilge. The space has filled with water, and George has run out of air. The sailor falls to the floor, gasping, shaking his head no, and pounding the wet floor.

"Sooner! I should have found that hole sooner! God damn it!"

"We can seal off this full section!" Victor assures him. "Come on. We can at least seal off this and a couple of the other passages. Let's move!"

Climbing up to the middeck, hands pressing against the tilting walls for support, Victor passes near his own bunk. He suddenly remembers the beautiful wooden puzzle boxes. Running back to the room, he drops to one knee and pulls them out from their hiding place. If this ship ends up going down, and God help them all if it does, he wants to take the boxes with him when he abandons ship.

He slings the sack over his shoulder. Back in the companionway, he and George race to lock all available hatches.

"This should have been done sooner!" Victor shouts.

"The captain never ordered it!"

"Fuck him."

The steel of the ship may have flexed slightly. One of the hatches won't latch anymore. Dropping to their knees, they try to force the metal door into place.

A low rumble suddenly shakes the ship.


Down in the engine room, the water has climbed high enough to make the ship list another five degrees. As this happens, the accumulated water sloshes to one side where it suddenly reaches and cools the bottom curve of one of the heavy boilers. In an instant, the stressed metal at the bottom cools and rapidly contracts while the rest of the boiler remains hot.

With a terrible pop and hiss, the boiler blows out one of its side seams, sending rivets flying. One of the rivets blasts right through Johnny C.'s left shoulder. He kneels into the water, holding the wound. His screams are lost in the roar of the escaping steam.

With a grimace Johnny C. sinks beneath the dark water as the ship continues to tip. The second boiler blows shortly thereafter. The hot water rushes out, flattening out along the floor, mixing with the other water and heating it until the room feels like a warm bath.

The *Gossamer* is not coming back up now, not with all this water piled inside. The next wave pushes the freighter further off its centerline, and Victor bangs his head again, this time against the wall of the companionway. His world turns gray.


There comes a point in any marine tragedy that can be called the point of no return. This may happen when a list becomes too severe or when the waves become too high. Sometimes it happens when several smaller problems stack up to the point where, together, they merge into one huge problem that cannot be overcome. With the rupturing of its boilers, the *Gossamer* reaches its point of no return. Its list becomes a slow, steady tip. The lack of power, because the boiler is gone, means the captain can no longer steer amidst the waves. The crests of the breaking waves finally shove the vessel too hard, turning her completely on her side and even beyond.

The starboard paddlewheel, which is now facing the sky, starts to pinwheel freely. There is enough steam still in the pipes to feed its piston, but it has no real power. The wheel is nothing more than a spinning flower decorating a grave.

The keel starts to move down again. For an agonizing minute the optimists in the crew believe she might recover. The *Gossamer* is quite seaworthy after all. She has survived a good battering during other crossings. She's weighted well too. She might right herself—given enough time. But there is no such luxury. Another wave slaps directly into the exposed top deck. Then another. Finally, the pounding whitecaps tear the main hatch away like a lid from a cheap tin can. The force literally pivots the ship around its huge, buried portside paddlewheel. At the same time the starboard wheel is ripped completely off, housing and all. It floats off over the waves like a giant straw boater hat.

The sea rushes in hard, and the *Gossamer* will never sit upright again.

Victor sloshes and rolls in the dark companionway, trying to force himself out of his daze. He knows he has to climb up to the deck.

As he struggles to stand, the incoming water pushes a loose footlocker along in front of it, hitting him in the chest. His breath blasts out and he fights to get it back. The companionway fills quickly. Can he swim out? No. He lacks the breath to do that. If only he had the air. If only. The boat starts to roll over, upside down now. He loses his sense of direction and finds himself sliding back into the crew quarters, all the way back near his bunk. He finally finds an air pocket near the floor, which has suddenly become the ceiling. The ship groans. He thrusts his head into the air pocket and breathes greedily. Coughing and gasping, his heart pounds. Lack of oxygen. Cold. The thought of trying to swim back down the companionway frightens him. But he must do it. He has to.

He takes a big breath and prepares to dive, but he hears the ladder to the main hatch rip loose, followed by the sound of the hatchway itself groaning and folding. He hears another noise too, louder and more intense. It's an otherworldly groan that shakes the *Gossamer* to its core. Victor can't quite see it, but in his mind he pictures either the main smokestack, or perhaps the stubby mast, slowly being bent over.

Like a giant lever, the mast pries at the deck as it falls, twisting and contorting all the metal beneath it. That includes the ceiling of the companionway nearest to Victor. The entire space folds down, sealing itself tighter than a lid on a garbage can.

For the first time, Victor deeply panics. He has to find a way out. But there is no time left. He pounds at the metal walls until his knuckles bleed.

He looks toward the only opening in the room. The porthole. It's way too small for a ship of this size. Why didn't the ship's architect see that! A crewman could never fit thought it. Victor certainly will not fit through it. But the puzzle boxes … at least they might be able to float free. Victor turns to look behind him. Even in the darkened room, even through the water, he can see the floating sack that he had been carrying just minutes before. His stomach tightens.

Victor slaps and tugs at the dogs on the bottom of the porthole. They slowly unscrew. Prying them away, he yanks at the glass with his bleeding fingernails. More water rushes in as it opens, but so what? Water doesn't matter anymore. Nothing matters now.

Strangely, he starts to feel at peace with that part of it. Somehow, knowing there is nothing more he can do removes the sense of panic, and releasing the boxes gives him a sense of purpose. It lets him hold all the horror around him at bay.

Hand feeling around inside the sack, Victor also thinks about his other wooden boxes—the big crates up on the deck. He wonders if they are light enough, with their equipment inside, to float free. And what about the other items he tossed inside? Would anyone be lucky enough to find them?

He tugs the puzzle boxes out of the sack, and he thinks about how this—all of this dreadful chaos—becomes part of the risk when you cross the ocean. You know catastrophe lurks. You accept the danger because, odds are, such a tragedy won't happen to you. If something does go wrong, you try to save yourself if you can. But if everything fails, you simply accept your fate because you spun the roulette wheel. You took the gamble and this time, this one time, you aren't one of the lucky ones.

Victor forces his hands toward the porthole. Shoving hard against the flowing water, he forces Johnny C.'s puzzle box out first. It immediately rises and disappears. The ship lurches back onto its side. The porthole is now pointing straight up and the ship is totally underwater. Victor kicks hard to keep himself near the small window. The air pocket he had relied on suddenly bubbles away through the open hole. No air left. Victor pauses for a moment, kisses his own box goodbye, and shoves it through the port.

He hears the swearing and the crying somewhere behind him, probably in the crushed companionway. Then he hears voices above him at the surface of water, muffled like they're shouting through a thick pillow. Those must be the voices of the lucky few who managed to abandoned ship. They are the ones who will ride the waves in stomach-churning rises and falls.

His task complete, Victor leaves his arm hanging out of the porthole. It feels like he's waving good-bye to the watertight box as it floats upwards. Or maybe he's waving farewell to the light? In spite of the dark storm clouds, he can still see some light up there beyond the surface. So far away. It really is beautiful, isn't it? His father always said that it was.

Good old bearded Eli Marius always had said a day of living was more important than any job he might have, or any problem he might face. Eli said days were meant to be enjoyed. Life was a party.

Victor had never understood his father. Now suddenly, as everything drifts away from him, he understands. His father had many friends. Victor, being all business and work ethic, has very few.

And now that sky. That water. That world. All gone, and never truly explored or deeply enjoyed.

The water darkens. Is that happening because the surface is now so far away? Or is it just the lack of oxygen? Victor doesn't care. A dead man's peace awaits him as the *Gossamer* heads toward the bottom. Arm still outstretched, Victor reaches toward the fading light.

It remains elusive.

Sometimes the ocean chooses to consume, rather than give, and this is one of those times.

The wrong place. The wrong time. The wrong choice.

Just that quickly, Victor Marius has left the party.

# Chapter 8

## *Rebel Remains*

*Sullivan's Island, Charleston, South Carolina*

*June 18, 1891*

It's barely eight in the morning, and temperatures at the shoreline near Charleston already have climbed past ninety degrees. A fifty-year-old woman stands near Branch Inlet southeast of the city. She softly tugs at her cotton blouse's high white collar. It's a discreet action that allows a little heat to escape from inside her clothes while she still maintains the prim formality expected from a proper Southern lady.

But, lady or not, the man she talks to while standing at the water's edge does not look at all like a gentleman. His shoes are scuffed and shabby. It's been three days or more since his face has seen a razor. His clothes—dark pants, light blue shirt, and a gray summer jacket—look expensive, yet they're a good twenty-five years out of fashion. An older cut with a longer coat. His pockets bulge, and the handle of a cheap knife tilts forward from inside his coat.

"Well, thanks for seeing me off," the shabby man mumbles to the woman. "I wasn't expecting that I'd ever see you again."

"No need to avoid it. And you know why I've come, Devlin. I still don't understand why you're heading north, and I'm here once again to try to talk you out of it. You've always hated the North, especially those wretched cities,

New York and Boston. They're absolutely full of the very people you hate."

The man shrugs. He just looks toward a blue dory waiting at the end of a short dock. The little boat, and the young sailor tending the oars, belong to an eighty-eight-foot steamer anchored at the far side of the island, near the mouth of Charleston Harbor. The ship, captained by a childhood friend of Devlin's, is a speedy contract carrier that transports cargo and U.S. mail up and down the East Coast. It visits most of the major cities between Boston and Savannah. At full steam, it can make it from South Carolina to Massachusetts in just under five days.

"I told you already, Kate. It's just something I have to do. You know that. I've tossed it around in my head and talked about it for years."

"I know you have, Devlin, but I've never liked the sound of it. It's bad blood. Sour grapes. I've told you and told you. Sometimes you just have to let things go."

"I don't know what you mean."

"Oh, I think you do." She touches his arm. It's the guiding touch of an older sister, not a friend or a lover. Yet Devlin has long avoided her guidance. He takes a step back, and her hand drops to her side.

"Listen," he says, "Clayton is waiting for me. He's already breaking the rules just by letting me aboard. I'm not going to keep him waiting."

She steps forward again, pleading with him, reaching for his broad shoulders. "You can't go. You can't do this! Please! That's why I came here this morning. All this anger of yours. All this resentment you have. You've had it for twenty-five years, and it's gotten you nothing. Aren't I correct? Nothing but a black heart."

"You're talking foolishness. I'm just going there for … well, for business. Two months, tops." He starts to step into the dory. As she watches him, she rolls up her sleeves, both to cool herself and to do something with the anxiety that's building up inside.

"If father could see you now," she shouts, "he'd be ashamed. Ashamed, Devlin!"

Devlin Richards turns suddenly. Not quite leaving the dory, he points a finger at her. "What did you say?"

"You heard me."

He squints in anger. "If our father was here, he'd be proud of me, woman! Damn proud. He'd see a man who's a fighter. A man who has decided finally to retake control of his destiny. That's what he'd see." He looks his sister up and down with a sneer. "And that's more than I can say about you!"

She glares at him and starts to fix her hair. She's already lost the battle against the day's humidity, and now just struggles to keep her composure.

"Nothing to say about that?" Devlin laughs. "You've managed to regain your status. You're looking right prosperous lately, Kate. But how did you to that? By marrying a Yankee? Think our daddy would be proud of *that*? No, my dear. You are the one he'd be ashamed of."

She looks him in the eyes, hurt, then looks away.

"You pretend that the rest of your family is on board with your decisions, Kate. Well, most of us ain't. Hell, I'm the only one in the family who even talks to you anymore. Have you noticed that?"

Kate's glare hardens into an icy stare. Devlin removes his foot from the dory, turns, and takes a couple steps toward her.

"Did you think we wouldn't notice that the lumberyard owned by that precious Yankee husband of yours imports wood from the North and the West? Hell, he even imports from Mexico. But he never buys anything from the loggers who work right here in the Carolinas. Why is that? Is it because your husband is just another damn Yankee, Kate? Spends more time looking out for other Yankees than he does for his townsfolk? He's just here to take what he can from us while putting the screws to what's left of the old Confederacy, even after twenty-five years."

Kate speaks to him through clenched teeth. "That's nonsense. What's done is done, and I know that my Edger is a good man. You hear me? And as for me, I did what I had to do to restore a good name to this family. To bring some level of success back to us. You need to remember that, Devlin. You used to have a good name once too."

Devlin laughs out loud. "A good name? We never had a God damn good name!" He spits at the sand. "Oh yes, you love to remember Father and the old homestead fondly, don't ya?" Behind him the sailor shifts uneasily in his seat, but Devlin continues speaking to Kate. "You've got some nice little storybook picture in your head about what things were like when you were a little girl. Don't you? Perfect family we had, eh? But you conveniently filter out the bad parts. You forget where all the old family money came from." He walks right up to her, finger pointing at her chest.

55

"You know what our father did for a living! Hell, Kate, you know what our whole family did, and we did it for three generations."

"We were planters!" Kate responds. "We had rice fields! And some tobacco growing in the valley." She shouts it with pride. But Devlin makes a sweeping gesture toward a dirt road behind her.

"We had a little pissant farm, Kate! A little food for ourselves and the servants. That's not where the family fortune came from. We bought and sold niggers. That's what our family did for years, and you know it. That's where the money came from. But you can't even make that word pass your lips, can you? Go on! Try to say it!"

He walks around her as she looks at the clouds. "Come on and say it, Kate. Our daddy was a slave trader! He owned two ships! He also owned one of them squares of land downtown that was used for slave auctions. You know all that. It's what paid for your petticoats and bonnets when you were a girl."

He sees her tense and close her eyes. But he continues just the same. "That's right. Fresh nigger flesh, sold into the fields nearly every week."

Kate turns away, hands over her ears.

"And that's why our family took the hardest hit of all, Kate. Twenty-five, no, twenty-six years now! A whole generation has passed since the end of that bloody war. Look around you. Other businesses around here eventually were rebuilt. This city has ships, docks, and cotton mills and sugar warehouses. But not our business! Oh no, not *our* dirty little family business. Our kind of trade was gone for good, wasn't it? And our family never prospered again."

Devlin holds his hands above his head and turns in a slow circle. "Now look at me, sister. Just look right close! Do I look like a man who was able to recover when the family business went to hell? Hum? Do I look like I was able to rebuild?"

Kate snarls at him. "The business you speak of was never one that I was proud of. So why should I care if it never came back?"

"Maybe you don't. But I sure as hell care, Kate. Because we lost everything. Even the farm. Just a long, slow decline for the Richards family, wasn't it? Hell yes, it was. Took us a long time to accept that." He squints at her, and she can see the great festering anger in his eyes. "Well, I'm sick of being on the downside of it, Kate. And I know whose fault it is."

"It's no one's fault. It was just the end of an era. A move on toward other things for everyone."

His voice drops to a whisper. "Is that what you think? That what you tell your Yankee husband? You know damn well whose fault it was! You saw the blue army come through. Three of them boys held you down and had a right nice bit of fun with you, Kate. Don't you remember that? The rest of us in the family sure remember it."

"You!" she seethes. "You promised to never speak of that. Years ago you promised me!"

"Yes, but it's just you and me out here today, sister, and that oarsman over there who will never see you again. I know you're angry too. We all are. We just keep it hidden.

Keep it tucked away inside because it's not good for business."

Kate looks down at the ground. "It's in the past, Devlin! What kind of business could you possibly have in the North since you hate them all so?"

He shrugs, returns to the rowboat, and starts to rearrange some bags that he's loaded into the bow.

"Our father would not be proud of you, you know," she shouts after him. "Look what's in your hand! Just look at it!"

Devlin looks down. In his hand is a large carpetbag.

"What are you planning?" she demands. "What are you going to do? Do you want to be like them? Is that it? Like those Yankees were when they came here?"

"Just business, my dear. That's all. Just doing a little trading with the good folks of New England. Is that so bad?"

He settles onto a wooden seat and gives her a little salute as the oarsman embarks.


*Something has fractured in you, Devlin.* Kate doesn't speak the words aloud, but she thinks them. *You're broken and you're someone I don't even know anymore.*

When the dory is about fifty feet from shore, Devlin tosses the empty carpetbag in front of the sailor. "See that? I took that off the first man I ever killed. Shot him dead when I found him in the burned out parlor of my house. That was quite some years ago. Guess I kept it as a trophy." He smiles an iniquitous smile as he holds the sailor's gaze.

The lad says nothing as he puts his back into his rowing.

"So, lad. Once we reach the mail ship, Clayton says it's just five days to Boston? Is that right? Think we can really make it there so fast?"

"I reckon that's about right, sir," says the beefy teenager, "if we don't hit no bad weather."

Boston. The very word gives Devlin a twitchy feeling in his stomach. Of all the Yankee cities, that one lurks as the absolute Yankee-est in his mind. It's the center of all that he sees as vile and inappropriately proper, Northern, and Yankee in the world.

And the insult that Massachusetts laid on South Carolina was particularly insidious in his eyes. They sent their offensive 54th Regiment to do battle with the sons of the South. Those were them damn colored troops. Them damn niggers, dozens and dozens of them with their silly blue uniforms and angry brown eyes.

It wasn't bad enough that the Yankees invaded his land, destroyed his family business and took all that he had. No, the Massachusetts folk had to compound that insult by doing what only a whorish state like theirs could do. They organized the black men, the very foundation of the Richards family business. Those Yankees, they trained them and then they sent them here to help ruin everything.

Everything.

Devlin looks the sailor up and down.

"Where you from, boy?"

"Atlanta, sir."

Devlin nods. "All right then. I guess you know the story then, don't ya? Happened a few years before you were born,

I suppose. But what they did to your town and your kin ... well, I guess you very well know how I feel about them Yankees."

The boy nods hesitantly. "Before my time. But, yes sir. I reckon I do."

Devlin looks out to sea. "They took it all from me, lad. From me and my family. I was just twelve years old when that war started. Living the good life. Next thing you know I was sixteen and wearing a bloody gray uniform. Still wore it when the whole mess ended."

The young man nods.

"They took it all away from us twenty-six years ago, boy. Every damn bit of independence and pride. A man doesn't forget something like that, especially if it never comes back to him."

"No sir. I bet he don't."

Devlin gets a vacant look as he talks. He looks toward the spit of land ahead of them and waits for them to round that point so that they can see the ship.

"A man tries to recover from something like that for a long time, boy. Thinks that maybe just a few more years is what it will take. But if it don't ever come back, part of you has to blame the people that took it. Ain't that right? You just be true and go ahead and place the blame where it belongs. Nothing wrong with that at all."

"No sir, I guess there ain't. Lots of folks have trouble letting things be, even now." The lad rows for a bit, then adds, "I seen it myself. Just like you say. My uncles and some of my neighbors. They all lost stuff. Family and farms and money. Some folks down in Atlanta never got their homes built back up again after they was burned. Years later, some of them, well, they's still kinda lost. They seem as bad in the head as them soldiers who came home after seeing too much blood. Them there folks, they live. They drink. They walk around looking into the distance. Just sort of existing."

The lad puts his back into the oars again as the ship comes into view. Devlin looks down and nudges the carpetbag with his toe. He makes a silent vow to himself that he's not going to come back home to Charleston until he's done with his *trading*. That's what he's calling this. His trading mission. He deserves a full bag. No one can say that he doesn't.

# Chapter 9

## *Flotsam*

Long slow squeak.

It's still dark when the shed door announces its movement like a trumpet call.

Amanda isn't sure if an hour has passed, or much more. She lies still and mouse-like under her tarps. She hears a scurry of human feet inside the shed. She dares not move as more than one hushed voice drifts over her hiding place.

"Try over there," one voice says. She hears hands paw through the coils of ropes that hang from the far wall.

From outside she hears the soft click of a bridle as a horse mutters its discontent.

"Find anything?" The voices have become a bit bolder. They believe the shack to be abandoned.

"Yes. I think so," It's a young man's voice. "There's something here we can use to fix it. Just give me a minute!"

Outside a man makes a clicking sound with his mouth. She can hear him leading the horse right up to the door. The morning air is so still that the sound of animal's foul horse breath seems to fill the room. Amanda thinks it best to remain totally motionless. She won't even peek out from beneath her canvas to see what's happening. Soon there's the sound of a horse collar being adjusted, then a stern voice as the horse starts to fight it.

"All right there! Easy, boy, easy! I know it's early. Settle down …." She can hear a buckle being cinched.

"You coming, William?" This time it's a woman's voice calling from outside.

"Yes, yes! I said I was. Just a minute!"

The young man still fiddling with the ropes in the shack is standing barely four feet from Amanda. "I just need to find the right length. I can't believe that damn strap broke. Of all the times!"

"Just take anything!" the man outside says. "We'll make it work. If we don't hurry up, we're going to miss everything. Others will get there first!"

"I can see others on their way up the road," the woman adds. "Come on now, Richard. Be quick!"

"I'm looking, all right?"

Amanda hears one other voice outside the barn. That makes four in all, three men and a woman. From the give-and-take of their conversation, she guesses they're all from the same family. As the young man exits the shack, he too starts to work on the horse collar.

Amanda waits a full two minutes, then figures it's safe to sit up, even though she still hears them outside.

The urgency in the family's voices tells her this isn't just the start of another workday for them. These people are interlopers in the shack, just like her. They seem to be on their way to something important—something that apparently has put them in a race with others.

*What in the world is going on?* Amanda thinks to herself as she creeps to the small windows. The people gathered to fix the horse collar are too preoccupied to see or hear her.

"Go bareback if you have to, William!" one of the men shouts. "We need to get out there right now!"

"Blast it!" William responds. "We're going to need the wagon, ain't we? Well, ain't we? Then stop talking and let me fix the damn lead!"

The woman gasps as she looks down the road. "How did so many people find out?"

"Well, people talk," William says as he works. "I hear tell that things have been washing ashore since midnight. Stuff is all over the place. Cousin Eddie said there's already people picking through the sand from Nauset all the way down to the Chatham Light!"

The woman looks over the men's shoulders. "William! Please!"

"All right! I've got it." Standing a bit back from the window, Amanda watches William lead the horse in a half circle. The four people climb aboard, and the wagon slowly rolls away. A moment later, she lets herself creep toward the door, carefully peeking out before venturing into the open air.

The woman, whoever she was, had been quite correct. Amanda sees others on the road. Many others. A parade of townsfolk is a strange sight just before daybreak. They look like confused lemmings heading toward the sea.

The rain has slowed to almost nothing, and the sky has started to clear. Slipping out the door, she flees over a dune, slipping into a scrubby thicket of dune grass and squatting low. Waiting for another wagon to pass, she slips through the grass and makes her way back onto the path. At this point it's little more than a winding ditch curving down a gradual slope.

There are people on horseback, in wagons, and on foot. They talk in whispers. She recognizes a face or two from town, but there's no one she knows well. No one pays her any mind as she merges and walks along with the parade. Most of the people seem to be coming from Chatham and East Orleans and probably points beyond. They snake out through a flat area, and up ahead she can see them descending a dune.

As Amanda reaches a narrow point in a path, she hears a hissing, clanking, steaming noise behind her. Stepping to the side, she spies a strange-looking cart coming up the ditch.

Amanda has only seen photos of horseless carriages before. They are rare as hen's teeth, and she's heard stories about people racing out of their houses just to catch a glimpse of one. Now, one is coming at her, and the hissing, snarling contraption scares her.

Other people react the same way, stepping out of the way and stopping to stare as the steam car sputters down the path. As it draws close, Amanda realizes the thing looks far different from any picture she's seen. First of all, it's huge. It must be twenty feet long and seven feet high. Rather than rubber tires or even traditional wagon wheels, this cart has huge solid wooden wheels that are four feet in diameter. They look like thick tavern tables turned on their sides. The front of the vehicle looks more like a mini version of a locomotive than a carriage. It has a fat black smokestack rising from a boiler tank. Along the edge of the stack sits a brass steam whistle. Amanda suspects it could pierce her eardrums should the driver elect to pull its chain.

It is, basically, a small train built to run without a track. Its front wooden wheels pivot slightly left or right, allowing it to make gradual turns. As it pulls past, she spies a small plaque on the side of the boiler that says "Dudgeon."

As it descends the slope, the engine starts to sputter a bit. In a matter of seconds, the whole contraption hisses to a stop. The driver lifts his goggles, and Amanda can see that he's a thin, pale older man. A woman of roughly the same age, possibly his wife, is seated beside him.

"Great! Look at this now," the woman huffs. "I told you we shouldn't have taken this silly thing! We should have just used the horses and the wagon! We'll never get there."

"Silence!" the man warns, but his voice sounds more amused than threatening. "It's just the silly valve again. It's still sticking. I can fix it in two minutes."

He steps out and hurries to the front of the hulking wagon. Amanda walks alongside. He nods quietly to her and fiddles with something deep inside the machinery.

"Do you need help?" Amanda asks.

"No ... no, my dear ... well ...."

She hears a soft clank.

"Well ... yes, actually. Maybe if you just hold your hand right here. Careful now! Hot hot!" He moves her hand to the side. "No, no. Right here." He places her fingers around a small bar that runs the length of the engine. "That's it."

The woman inside the wagon leans forward to see what's going on.

"Agnes! Turn that big valve on the dash about halfway back!"

As the two women handle their assigned duties, the man walks to the other side and bangs on a pipe. There is a new hiss and a sputter. "Now, young lady, pull!"

Amanda yanks the rod back and feels the wagon lurch.

"And there we go!" He walks back to the front of the auto and gives Amanda a smile. "This is a steam wagon, you know. Not one of those newfangled internal combustion engines! No, ma'am. It's old and very temperamental!" The bar she's holding grows hot, and Amanda pulls her hand away.

"Much obliged to you!" The old man climbs back in, opens the dash valve to its full extent, and pulls his dusty goggles back down.

"I know it's not far, but would you like a ride to the beach, young lady?" he shouts. "Or at least as close as we can get in this thing?"

Amanda studies the wagon with trepidation. "I don't know. I've never ridden on anything like this ... um ... what do you call them? An auto-mo-beel?" She pronounces the name like three separate words that don't quite belong together.

"Not sure you want to ride this one then," the woman says. "It's not really a horseless carriage at all. It's more like a junk pile."

"Hush!" says her husband with a brush of his hand. "This thing has been running fine for decades."

In addition to the pair of seats at front of the vehicle, there's a back area that looks like a farm wagon. This section has a low bench running along either side. Amanda pulls herself up and into the deck. She can see that the benches are covered with dried chicken guano.

"Sorry," the gentleman calls back, "she's been sitting in the barn for couple of years. I just got her running again last week."

Amanda elects to sit on the back gate instead. As they start to move, she studies her dusty shoes as the sandy road flies by beneath them.

Amanda has never felt this sensation before. The speed is faster than a full gallop. They must be moving at twenty-five miles per hour or more. It's terrifying, and every bounce makes her stomach lurch. She clutches the edge of the wagon just to keep from bouncing out.

The ditch opens out onto Pochet Neck, and the view beneath her shoes becomes sandy with a hint of shells. Looking toward the front of the wagon as it slows, she sees a long line of other people. The group stands on a small sandy knoll, looking out to sea. The old man steers the steam car onto a flat spot where other wagons are sitting.

On the eastern edge of the Pochet Neck, itself little more than a spit of dry land hanging into the brackish swamps near Little Pleasant Bay, there is a small bridge and a quick slope down to the Orleans end of Nauset Beach. Some of the people break for the line and start running. Up ahead there are arguments over who will take their wagons first across a group of planks that serve as a small bridge over a ditch.

Amanda leaps out when she hears whips cracking and tempers flaring.

"You go on if you'd like, dear," says the woman. "We may be here for a while."

"I'm not even sure where I'm going, or even why all these people are here!"

But Amanda's words are lost as the steam engine starts to act up again, hissing loud and steady from under the tank. The noise drowns out all other noises.

She walks ahead, crossing the ditch on foot. It's not until she approaches the steep beach and the crashing waves that she finally sees what has attracted this early morning crowd. There is something out in the water to the east. Rather, there are thousands of somethings.

Squinting against the golden glow of the rising sun, she can see huge waves, tremendous things that loom up to thirteen feet tall then fold in on themselves to hit the steep drop-off of the beach with a loud thud. These are the largest waves she's ever seen on this beach, driven, no doubt, by the recent storm. Mixed with those waves are many pieces of wood—broken parts of what might have been a ship. Beyond the junk bobbing on the closest waves, she sees barrels floating about 400 feet offshore. Crates too, she thinks. There are also pieces of mast and rails and thousands of other things, some recognizable and some not. All of these things ride on the foamy crests like some kind of exotic waterfowl. They seem to glow in the slowly brightening yellow light.

Amanda holds her breath, as if her breathing might somehow erase the view in front of her before she has a chance to fully understand it.

But others don't hesitate. They run toward the water's edge looking like dolls standing before the huge waves. They wade into the surf, oblivious to the danger. Some of the wagons finally make it across the tiny bridge, and their drivers skirt the edges of the low sand cliffs, whipping their horses onward and looking for the best place to park near the water. She also sees lone riders, many of them bareback. They race up and down the beach. Riders hop on and off, pulling things ashore. Examining. Keeping or discarding. If what they pull ashore seems valuable enough, they stay with their prize, looking around for someone to help them drag it away. In the short time that she stands there, Amanda sees impromptu teams forming. Women agree to watch piles of supposed treasure while groups of men—growing from twos into fours and then sixes—pool their efforts to gather all they can find.

Hypnotized, Amanda finally stumbles toward the water. She can see the rising sun directly behind the towering waves, illuminating anything that lurks within. With the help of the sunlight, she can see things lurking there in the water. Wonderful things. Not just the drifting wood and barrels from the shipwreck, but also the things that have lingered beneath waves for thousands of years. In the yellow light she also sees weeds and a pair of large fish and even a curious seal who follows a bobbing barrel toward the shore.

Nearby, a woman shouts to Amanda. She's looking for help because she has speared a cargo net with a long stick. She appears to be trying to drag the net ashore, but it's too heavy. Amanda sees that some loose clothing and a broken crate are tangled in its ropes. "Can you help?" she calls out.

"Yes," Amanda nods. "Of course." She shouts her answer at the top of her voice, yet the words seem lost in the crashing surf. Just as she reaches the woman's side, a huge white oak beam from the shipwreck suddenly appears at the top of a wave. The next wave topples it end over end, and it crashes to a stop right next to them.

They give each other a nervous glance, and then together they heave and count and heave together, eventually dragging the net onto the shore.

The woman introduces herself as Faith. She reaches under her skirt and pulls a long kitchen knife out from the top of her stocking. She laughs aloud when she sees Amanda's surprised look.

"Last time I came out here to a shipwreck was about five years ago," Faith says with noticeable pride. "That experience taught me that a scavenger isn't much good without a knife. You need some kind of pry bar too. So we remembered to bring one of those too this time." The woman, whom Amanda judges to be about forty, nods up the beach. "My husband's got the pry bar up there."

Amanda looks down at the net as Faith cuts through one rope, then another. "Is that what we are?" she asks. "Scavengers?"

"Well, I'd have to say yes. Wouldn't you?" Faith comments with a sly smile. "But it's okay, dear. If it t'wernt us doing the taking, others would come along and grab it for themselves. When things like this wash up? Well, it's all too valuable to just leave on the beach. Finders keepers, eh?"

As the woman slices through each rope, Amanda helps strip back the pieces of the net. "But, is it okay to do this?"

Amanda wonders aloud. "I mean, doesn't the ship owner have salvage rights? Or maybe the family of the crew or something?"

Faith laughs. "Well, I don't know the law, dear. But I do know this beach will be picked clean by noon. All this stuff will be gone before word even makes it to the outer cape that pieces of a wrecked ship have come ashore."

The woman waves her knife to emphasize her point, and Amanda is struck by the absurdity of the image. Any other day, it's likely that Faith would be the very image of a proper church-going woman, a farmer's wife who is not much different from what Amanda herself might be in seventeen years or so. Yet this prim and proper woman is now wet to her waist, hair undone and cheeks smudged, holding a knife and looking like a she-bear huddled over a fresh kill. Amanda senses some kind of primitive survival instinct at work, and she's surprised at how quickly such a thing can be triggered.

"Now dear," Faith ruminates, "you can go climb the dunes and wait for the police if you want. Or you can even wait for the lawyers and the insurance men. But I'll tell you what … there are people far less deserving than you and I out here. Should we stand back and let them help themselves? Or do you want to work with me to help gather up whatever we can claim?"

Faith smiles a wicked little smile. "Of course, that also means you end up helping yourself in the process." She winks and goes back to cutting. "Far as I'm concerned, you helped me haul this out. Half of what we find in here is yours."

They pull a long cotton jacket out first. It looks wet but brand new. Faith speculates that it was probably part of the cargo, not something that belonged to the crew. "My husband can use this. That is, if the water hasn't shrunk it too much." She studies Amanda. "Is that okay with you, dear?"

"Yes, I mean … I guess so." If Faith wants the jacket, she can certainly have the jacket. Amanda isn't really sure what sort of claim she has to this, or to anything else that might wash up.

"Well, come on! You helped drag it out. See what else is in the pile!"

Amanda reaches out and pulls a rubber-coated slicker from the tangle. It doesn't look like anything fancy. In fact, it looks homemade, like someone just poured melted rubber over a cloth coat to make it more waterproof.

"Now that's interesting, dear," the older woman said. "Doesn't look very new. That might have belonged to one of the sailors. Check the pockets."

"I couldn't …."

"Oh, go on, go on. It's like gambling, dear, except that you don't have to risk any of your own money to be a winner. Reach in. See what you find!"

Amanda searches for a pocket opening and inserts her hand. She squeals and quickly yanks it back out. Laughing, she pours out some seawater, along with a handful of very tiny minnows. Trying again, she pulls out a handful of coins, some fishing twine wound around a sliver of wood, and a single dollar bill.

"There you go!"

She quickly checks the other pockets, mesmerized. She finds some more coins, a scrap of a nautical chart, and, in a large inside pocket—jackpot!—a shiny brass compass.

Amanda smiles with delight and holds it up, but Faith pulls Amanda's hand back down and whispers conspiratorially.

"First rule of scavenging, dear, keep your finds to yourself. Last time out here, I saw someone claim that they dropped the thing that another person had just found. But I know that wasn't true. I've seen fights break out over silly things. My advice? Just keep quiet about all things, and you'll do fine."

Faith slips the compass and coins into the front pocket of Amanda's damp house dress, giving it a pat. "You just keep that right there, you hear?"

Soon they're on hands and knees pawing through the rest of the cloth in the net. They find another dollar, a needle and some thread. Another coat. Not much else.

A man on a horse rides up and fastens a rope to the large beam. He pulls it toward the path, telling Amanda and Faith that he plans to build a new barn, and this will make a nice center support.

Faith wades out toward a tangle of planks, but a commotion down the beach makes everyone stop. They look toward the gathering crowd. Someone is wailing. People run up, look over the shoulders of others, then turn their heads away with a gasp.

"Oh Lord," says the man on the horse. "Looks like they found one." He unhitches his rope and rides toward the crowd.

"One what?" Amanda calls after him.

"A sailor," he shouts. "A body!"

She sees someone reach toward the sand and flip a lifeless form over on its back. The crowd takes a step back.

It is too terrible to think about, yet she follows the others. She looks at the backs of the people, then moves closer as first one then another turns away. Someone vomits into the water. The woman directly in front of Amanda finally steps back, hands squeezing her temples like she wants them to erase the image she's just seen. Amanda steps up and immediately finds herself growing dizzy, hand covering her mouth.

She looks into a bleached white face, its eyes open and empty of everything except grains of wet sand. The dead sailor faces the clouds but sees nothing. Then she notices that only part of his face is white. The edges are greenish, and the chin has been worn down to a meaty, brown, flat spot, probably from being dragged over the sand and rocks all night by the waves. His shirt is open, and the rest of his body looks shiny white too. Amanda looks away, looks back, then looks away again. She stumbles back as others push in to take her place. It's a morbid yet irresistible sight. A freak show on the beach.

Away from the crowd, she sits down hard, fingers finding the compass in her pocket. She feels Faith's hand on her shoulder.

"Nothing you can do, dear. Act of God, you know."

"I know."

Amanda closes her eyes. When she opens them again, she sees a man searching through the dead sailor's pockets.

"But, look at him! To just take that poor sailor's things," she whispers to Faith. "It doesn't seem right. None of this does."

The woman sits in the sand beside her. "Well, think of it this way. Think of the dead as being able to give something to the living—even after they're gone. Does that make sense?"

Amanda says nothing.

"I know, I know dear. It sounds like I'm justifying all of this. But none of us farm folks are in great financial shape. Especially out here on this godforsaken spit of land. Look at this place. It's a sandy wasteland that stretches far out into the dark cold ocean. This cape is curved like a huge arm that's reaching for death itself."

Then Faith gestures toward the water. "Did you know the Pilgrims first landed out here on the cape? Yes, right out at the end, several days before they went to Plymouth. Everyone likes to say that Plymouth was where the Pilgrims reached America. They've got plaques there, and that silly rock and everything. But the Pilgrims first stepped onto America way out by Provincetown. But they thought the land here was bad. Too sandy. Not right for farming. So they moved on." Faith laughs, picking up a handful of sand and letting it slide through her fingers. "Yet here we are, all of us, trying to farm this land anyway. Trying to survive off this lousy soil that even the Pilgrims didn't want."

Amanda picks up some sand too. "Wayne says the soil is good where we are. He says the crops are good some years— a lot of years, really."

"That your husband? Wayne?"

Amanda nods.

"But he's not here with you."

"No." She hesitates then says, "And I'm glad of that."

The two women exchange knowing glances.

"No. It's not easy out here, dear. Not easy for any of us."

Gazing out over the wreck, Faith says, "These sailors were hardworking men, like our husbands mostly try to be. These sailors probably were men who took care of their own." She kicks at the coats in front of them. "I think, in some small way, it would make them smile to know they're still helping someone out. They have a legacy that lives on because folks like us have come down here to pull the pieces of their lives out of the water. I think it's better if someone finds these things than to just let them wash ashore and rot."

It takes some coaxing, but Amanda again ventures to the water's edge. Again she collects the flotsam of the shipwreck. There are indeed things of value bobbing here and there. She drags out a barrel of salt pork for which someone offers her three dollars, right on the spot. She agrees to the sale. She watches as a group of men pull out a section of a wooden rail with a polished plank still screwed to its side. Gold letters spell out the name *Gossamer*. A small blue butterfly is carved next to the letters.

Amanda and Faith return several times to the surf, wading in to their waists, dragging out several wooden crates. Faith runs to find her husband and returns with his pry bar. It's just an old piece of black pig iron, made straight and pounded to a point at one end. It's strong enough though, and the women use it to force open the crates, finding more cotton coats, a nice load of full beer bottles, which they also sell for a dollar fifty, and a crate with a lumpy canvas sack that has tiny brownish-gray stains at the bottom. It looks like a laundry bag, they agree, but why would it be in a crate?

Faith looks about nervously, then pulls the sack open. Inside are several items wrapped in tissue paper. The first is a glass plate. The second is a silver spoon. The third is a wooden picture frame with a photo of a sailor.

"Looks like the contents of a woman's hope chest!" Amanda says.

"Or a man bringing things home ... to help his sweetheart fill her hope chest."

They look at each other.

"Former sweetheart," Amanda whispers grimly.

Slowly, they unwrap the other items, tucking them in pockets and under their dresses. The final tally: four of each place setting, some solid silver spoons and forks, plus some other loose pieces. There are four larger plates too, with only a few chips, and a teapot, though not a whole tea set. The tarnish is terrible, accelerated by the seawater. The stains on the bag were created from the tarnish, leeching out of the silver like dark paint.

"Do you think these can ever be polished up again? Or are they ruined?" Amanda asks.

"I don't know. Maybe they can be saved. They haven't been in the water all that long."

The picture frame is cracked. Not just the glass, but the wood too. Cracked right through. But they keep it anyway, almost as a memento of the mystery owner of the moderately valuable items.

After prowling around a bit more and finding very little, Faith announces that she has to go home. There's canning to do. And her husband's brother is due to visit in two days. There's laundry, and house cleaning.

She offers Amanda a ride home, but the young woman doesn't answer.

"Not ready to go yet, dear? So what ARE you doing out here all alone?" She studies Amanda's eyes. "Did you even tell your husband that you were coming?"

"I didn't even know there was a shipwreck," Amanda admits. "I live south of the village. I was heading out here this morning to do some thinking."

"Running away from something?"

"Maybe. I don't know. Avoiding things for now."

Faith taps the bulging pockets of Amanda's dress. "Let me give you a bit of advice then. No one knows what you've found here today. It's not much, but all these things have some value. Buy yourself something nice with it. Or save it for an emergency, whatever that emergency may be."

Amanda nods.

"The sea has many secrets, dear. Your husband doesn't need to know about this one."

They hug, and Faith heads back to the dunes, joining her husband and searching for the path to the road. Amanda walks north instead, along the shore ... until the crowds thin out and the water starts to look like a normal ocean again, with only a few scraps of wood floating here and there.

*An emergency,* she thinks. What exactly constitutes an emergency? Is an emergency what she's experiencing right now? Not yet. She still hopes to make her marriage work if she can. She has no alternative. She can't go back to Boston. That would seem like a big step in the wrong direction.

Her decision, for now, is that she will go back to the farm and try again. Wayne will yell. Then they'll make up and that will be that. There's so very much to do on a farm in the summer. The two of them will be too occupied for any real trouble to show its face.

Amanda kicks at the small pieces of shells as she walks. So many lives lost in this wreck. It's sad. And that makes the scavenging seem doubly brutal. But she's happy to keep her newfound trinkets.

Up ahead, she spots a clump of seaweed. It sits high, like it's bunched up on top of a small rock. She walks over, not really expecting to find anything, but half wondering what a rock is doing out here in the middle of a wide stretch of sand. Brushing the vegetation away, she sees that it isn't a rock at all. It's a small wooden box. Bigger than a glove box but smaller and squarer than a shoe box. Picking it up, she discovers it's actually highly polished wood, with scrolling and inlays of lighter and darker woods. How strange.

She turns the box over and over. It's lovely. Perhaps it's a jewelry box. Wouldn't that be a find? The water beads up on the oily wood. It looks practically new. The shipwreck and the water seem to have had little effect on it, save for a small scrape on one corner. Amanda tries to open the box, only to discover it doesn't have a handle or clasp. She looks for hinges and finds none. Yet the box seems hollow—at least partially. She can see a seam. Perhaps the top just slides off? She tries, sliding it then pivoting it, but she can't make it budge. Several other attempts—poking, prodding, and pushing at the top and corners—also prove fruitless. Maybe it just needs to dry out. She shakes it and hears a couple distinct thumping sounds deep inside. There's also a gravel-like rattle in the lower part of the box.

She stares at the thing, frowning. It's not clear what this box is, but it's certainly worth keeping. Tucking it under her arm, she decides that it's finally time to head for home.

Walking slowly back down the beach, Amanda formulates a plan. She will be straightforward. She'll tell Wayne that she traveled out to the shipwreck this morning. That will be her excuse to explain her absence. She'll say she heard about the wreck, and then she'll show him the compass and a couple of the smaller things she's found. That should appease him. She'll hide the silver for a rainy day, just like Faith suggested.

What about the box? Should she show him that too? Wayne can be clever and he might be able to help her open it. But she decides to hide it away for now. Wayne is a man with little patience. If he's angry, he may very well just take his hammer and crack it open. That isn't Amanda's way. Dealing with something like this, whatever "this" may be, will take some time and a good deal of consideration.

# Chapter 10

## *Associates*

"I'll take the wheel for the next hour or so, lad. Why don't you take a little break?"

The young sailor steering the mail ship looks confused. He's been at his post since 10 a.m., and he had expected to work until midafternoon. But the sudden appearance of Captain Harkins on the bridge has brought with it a small change of plans.

"Sir?"

"You heard me, sailor. Be back in an hour."

"Okay. I mean, yes sir!"

With Devlin Richards at his side, the captain closes the wheelhouse hatch. He takes the wheel, and Devlin leans against the back wall.

"I do appreciate you giving me a ride north, Clayton. This is a fine way to travel."

"Aye, running a mail ship is good work," his friend says. "I enjoy it. The pay's good enough to keep the ship in top shape, and no one gives us much trouble. It's safe too. Anyone tries to mess with a mail ship, and they'll get the U.S. Navy jumping right down their throat."

Devlin nods. "Seems you're taking a bit of a chance then, bringing me on board."

Captain Harkins shrugs. "Not really. It's still my ship. I just contract to deliver the mail. Why? You're not a wanted man, are you?"

"Not officially. No."

"No more than me," Harkins winks. "Never got caught, did we, Dev? Never caught up to us for one damn thing." They both snicker.

"Boys will be boys," Devlin nods, looking out windows at the front of the bridge. "Lots of boys were doing what they could to survive back then. Not sure anyone really wanted to catch us, you know? Same as they didn't really want to catch them James boys up in Missouri."

The captain smirks at the comment. "Yeah, sometimes a little revenge is expected. Let the boys have their justice."

They chat for a while about the old days. It's been at least five years since their paths last crossed. In almost no time they settle into the relaxed conversation of two men who have been friends since childhood.

"That bag that you brought on board ...," Clayton inquires. "That what I think it is?"

Devlin doesn't answer.

"I can't believe you kept that! Kind of stupid, don't you think? Proof that you might have had something to do with that carpetbagger's disappearance."

"Oh, who cared about him? You certainly didn't."

"No, but I never expected you to kill him. I just wanted to rough the bastard up a little. Kick his ass down the road."

"So we got a little rougher than usual. Not like anyone ever missed him."

Clayton laughs.

"And now look at you." Devlin shakes his head. "All respectable and working for the damn U.S. government. Who'd have thought it?"

"Yeah. I know. Funny, isn't it? Them givin' money to an old rebel like me? I'm glad to take the work though. I charge them through the nose for these trips, and they don't even bat an eye."

"You're a lucky man, Clayton. Lucky indeed."

Capt. Clayton Harkin nods. "That I am, Dev. Guess I don't mind sharing a little of that luck with an old friend. That's why you're getting a free ride."

"I do appreciate it. I really do."

Harkins takes a deep breath, unsure how to approach a subject that's been lingering between them. "So, old friend, what are you dragging me into here? Not sure I still like being an accessory to your schemes. It tends to get dangerous for me, as I do recall."

"Not dangerous to you, Clay. I'll see to that. You're just providing a little transportation."

"It's going to have to be a one-way trip. After you've finished … well … whatever you plan to do up there, I'm not sure I want to be around you."

"I'll find my own way home. You don't have to worry about that."

Captain Harkins takes a compass reading then throws a loop of twine over the wheel. It will keep them on a steady course while he turns his attention elsewhere for a moment.

"Fair enough then. What can I do to help you? Besides this little ride?"

"You've spent time in Boston. Tell me what I need to know when I get there."

Clayton nods. "I can tell you a bit." He pulls out a small map that shows Boston Harbor.

"Well, here's what I can tell you. We'll land about here."

He points to the Lewis Wharf area.

"Now look up here. North of Boston there's a peninsula known as Charlestown. You've got the harbor on the east, the Mystic River on the north, and a navy yard sitting right between the two. Reason I'm telling you this is that there's all sorts of people coming and going in that neighborhood. Ships arriving. Sailors drinking and fighting. The police up there have plenty to keep their eye on. If you look like a reasonable man who's not there to cause trouble, they're not going to pay much attention to you."

The captain scratches an address on a piece of paper.

"A friend of mine runs a little place there, called The Rose Point Pub. His name is Johnson Aubrey. You want to buy and sell something, his pub is a good place to go. All sorts of business is conducted there. Looks like a hellhole, but you'll see rich and poor alike inside the door."

Devlin nods and takes the piece of paper.

"Hold on, let me give you another name too." He takes the paper back and thinks for a moment. "I feel strange passing this name along. I've made him some promises. It's not a good thing if people know who he is."

"So why is he so special?" Devlin asks.

"He's a cop. Not a bad one. Just hit some hard times a while ago. He understands business, and it's never a bad thing to have a friend on the police force."

"No," says Devlin. "Never a bad thing at all."

Clayton writes down just the officer's last name. *Hudson.*

"There. You don't needs his full name. Just keep an eye out for Patrolman Hudson. He walks a beat in the area around Boston's Chinatown and the south end of the Common. You get in trouble, maybe he can help. He knows the city. You need to do some kind of special business, he'll know where to go. Just be sure to give him a fair percentage."

"Chinatown, hmm? You know if he makes some of his money off the smoke?"

Clayton shakes his head. "Can't say, Devlin. I've said more than I should have already."

Devlin nods. "Not a problem. This is a good start. I do appreciate it."

Papers and maps are tucked away. Devlin offers the captain a hand-rolled smoke, and the two of them puff their cigarettes in silence. No matter how successful Devlin's trip is, it may be a long time before they see each other again.

# Chapter 11

## *The Bottom of the Trough*

Crooked sticks of light shine through unevenly spaced boards. The old barn never gets the attention it needs. The filtered light illuminates floating specks of dust stirred loose by restless animals. They're usually out to pasture by midday, but Wayne has forgotten to set them loose.

Amanda returns home—the barn very much serves as her home now—and she looks up through holes in the ceiling to see the underside of flattened tin cans. Temporary patches that ended up lasting years.

Sensing haste and tension within her, the animals fuss and retreat, save one eternally friendly cow. It's Jessie again who steps forward in greeting. Amanda slows and quickly strokes the cow's chunky white face and kisses its nose. Then she hurries on, clenched fists holding her skirts above her knees. The bunched cloth also serves as a makeshift sack containing her booty from the shipwreck.

The scent of horses invades her nostrils as she begins to climb. The old ladder to the loft has always bothered her, so trying to navigate it one-handed is nerve-wracking. The age of the wood is unknown. Left by a previous owner, it has nails tacked over nails with wire and tape holding together the split ends of the rungs. It's a losing battle against entropy, but still it holds.

Amanda doesn't weigh much. The wood survives. Once she's up in the loft, she feels safer. The ladder would not be so supportive of Wayne.

On hands and knees she searches for a place to hide her treasure. With half a smile, she passes hands under loose hay, mindful of sharp nails. Finding the right spot, she slides the silver toward the back. Then places the box in front of it, sprinkling loose hay over both. The compass and the folded dollar bills stay with her, tucked into an apron pocket.

Earlier, on her way back from the beach, Amanda had stood at the edge of the woods and watched Wayne leave for town. He called to her once, facing toward the barn. Then he left.

If typical patterns hold, he will be gone for several hours. So she has some time to herself. Satisfied that the box can be hidden here, she slides it back out from its hiding place and settles onto the floor of the loft. Hastily pushing some hay into a ball behind her, she leans back, the box resting between her knees in a sea of light-blue cotton. Its lacquered maple and ebony glisten in the soft light.

*What is this thing?*

It's not a shipping container. That much she knows. It's too small and fancy and hard to open. A quick shake tells her it doesn't contain shoes or foul tobacco.

She flips it over and over. Maybe it's a jewelry box. That's the most likely thing. And that could make this a wonderful treasure indeed. Yet, doubts linger. It's not like any jewelry box she's seen.

Amanda suddenly laughs out loud at herself. "How many jewelry boxes has a gutter flower like me actually seen in my life?" she says. "Two? Three? And how many of those were fine ones?"

A woman with no jewels to her name has scant experience judging what a nice jewelry box should look like.

Flipping and spinning it, she examines the cube but can find no hinges and no clasp. There's only the barest hint of a seam. She pries at the thin line with little luck. Finally she stops, setting the box on her knees, regarding it with amused bewilderment.

"What is this thing!?" This time she says it aloud.

The inlays on the surface create a swirling pattern. It looks vaguely oriental, but with other influences too. Maybe Greek. All the inlays seem to swirl around a central point, a raised diamond of wood set in the top of the box.

After staring at the swirls for several minutes, she senses that the design might actually be a hint. They accent and highlight the diamond shape, which is slightly darker. Perhaps that central wooden shape is the opening clasp she seeks, yet she can't slide her fingernails under it.

Angry, she picks at it until she feels slight movement. Frowning, she presses it down. Once it's depressed, she discovers she can slide the diamond toward the box's front. With a light click, the full top, perhaps a quarter inch thick, pops up. She's then able to swing the top open. The compartment below is also just a quarter-inch thick.

This most definitely isn't like any box she's seen before. What kind of a lid only unveils the top quarter inch of the container? The lid itself looks like a solid piece of wood, but she notices a small panel within the lid itself. Sliding that to the right, she sees a tiny bit of water leak out. There's a musty smell, and she finds a small amount of green slime on her fingers. She also sees some writing. Two notes are scrawled right on the wood itself.

The top note is written in beautiful flowing cursive. "This box has seven compartments and 27 moves. You've found the first one, but not all are obvious. Good luck. – V.M."

The second note, written beneath the first, is scrawled in a hurried hand. It reads: "June 17. We are near Georges Bank and taking on water. Terrible storm. May God forgive all of us. This box contains my last will and testament. If found, please ...." But the water has soaked the bottom part of the message, and the ink has washed away. That's all she can read.

Amanda feels a strong chill. It starts near her temples and travels down through her shoulders and stomach. Even her feet feel cold. She closes the lid for a moment, staring toward the barn door. The lines of illuminated dust still hover below.

She feels scared for some reason. What has she found? What obligation does she now have to the previous owner of this box? This seems so personal, more personal even than seeing that dead sailor on the beach. In her hand she holds someone's last moments. A last message. The pain of that poor sailor seems to live on inside the box along with the writing.

*May God forgive us all,* he wrote. For what? For dying? Or did he seek forgiveness for the way he and the others on that boat lived?

*What does a person think about when they know they're going to die?* She wonders. Perhaps V.M., whoever he was, sought forgiveness for some specific sin. Or for foolishness. Or maybe for missed opportunities and wrong choices.

She doesn't know, but she can imagine.

Closing her eyes, she tries to picture herself standing on the deck of a sinking ship. Breathing her last. Accepting the unacceptable. She tries to imagine her final thoughts and realizes they would indeed carry with them much regret.

Her fingers rest on the top of the lid, and they trace the smooth seams of the inlaid wood. The sensation against her fingers brings her back to the present. She notices for the first time that there's a piece missing. One of the inlaid sections of ebony is gone. No surprise, given what the box has been through.

Opening the lid again, she rereads the top paragraph. *Seven compartments and 27 moves.* This box isn't at all what she had suspected. It's not for jewelry. It may have started its life as some kind of toy, but that toy has been turned into a lifeboat that carries with it a sailor's thoughts and souvenirs. She finds this charming in a way, not only because it's something she's never seen before, but because, in the last moments of some sailor's life, he found a new purpose for a toy box and it became a legacy that he could leave behind. A time capsule.

So, what else is tucked inside?

*27 moves.* Pushing the diamond down must be the first move. So what else counts as a move? Is lifting the panel within the lid considered the second move, or is that still part of the first? And is that tiny slot big enough to be considered one of the seven compartments?

Amanda finds herself wishing for an instruction sheet so she can rush ahead, finding all the compartments and exploring every item that might be tucked inside.

Her hands trace the next layer of wood. It's rougher than the polished exterior and lacks the same fancy inlays. The wood feels oily, and she realizes it's teak, a wood she's familiar with from the decks and railings of ships back in Boston. The outside edge surrounding the teak looks like the same maple used in the exterior of the box. For five minutes she conducts a maddening search for a way into the next level. Feeling along the edges, she looks for a bump, a hole, a pin, anything. But there's no hint of how access is achieved. Frustrated, she turns it over, searching the bottom for an alternative entry point.

Thwarted at every turn, she considers finding a knife to pry up the teak. But that would damage the box. It's far too remarkable a thing to injure it. Besides, she's too stubborn to give up so easily.

She looks closer, prodding, scraping, and pressing. Okay … if the top held a hint of sorts, maybe there's something here that she's missing. Eventually she feels a slight give to the whole teak piece when she presses directly down on the top. She sets it on the floor of the loft and presses hard. The top sinks slightly and clicks. The release must be spring-loaded. When she lets up, the teak section pops up, and she can now grasp its sides. Spinning it counterclockwise, she literally unscrews the full board with a turn and a half.

The new compartment is also very shallow. Finding a piece of paper tucked inside, she unfolds it slowly. The seawater hasn't penetrated this far inside, but the paper shows slight stains from the teak oil. Pressing the paper flat on the floor, Amanda notices it's the same handwriting that scrawled the good-bye note. This time the text looks neater and less panicked. She guesses it was written sometime before the day the ship sank.

She has trouble making out the words in the dim light and decides to bring the whole box outside, where it's easier to see. She sets all the pieces into her lap. Gathering her skirt around them, she descends the ladder, resourcefully holding the folds of her skirts in her teeth so she can use two hands on the rungs.

Outside, she sits on the edge of the farm's watering trough. In the sunlight she can see that the note is actually a short poem.

### Emma's Lament

- Written at sea, June 15, 1892

*You left your soul out of its box*

*Accessible to the rain*

*Breathlessly you waited, Emma*

*For some sweet savior to come*

*And take from you*

*The silence called your life*

There's more text below this, but the teak oil has stained it, making it difficult to read. Amanda scans the words twice, not sure what to make of it. She knows nothing of poetry but suspects these stanzas don't fit any classic genre. It's written from the heart, not with a sense of classical style. It's more of a mournful thought scrawled late at night, scratched onto the back of what looks like an unused envelope. It's more emotion than story, arriving in moody rhythm, sans coherent phrasing. She pictures such words like angry animals clawing at the back of a sailor's mind. Maybe those words came when he was on night watch. Or maybe he was alone in his bunk.

She sees it as a poem to lost love. Maybe a death. But there's another thought here too. She traces a finger over the words.

"You left your soul out of its box," she reads aloud, "accessible to the rain."

Who thinks in images like that? The picture in her head both intrigues and disturbs her. Perhaps the woman, this Emma, was someone who felt too much, who longed too much, or even someone who might have been too passive in the face of … well … what? The author of this poem probably saw all of that in her.

Blinking, she refolds the paper. She doesn't really understand that sort of woman. One thing people have always told Amanda is that she's infinitely practical. Ever-resourceful. She certainly isn't the type who would worry about her soul—whether it's kept in the rain or someplace warm and dry. Amanda's soul seems fine and strong, thank you. Emma, whoever she was, must have been the type of fragile flower who never could have survived in the gutters.

Instead of worrying about Emma, Amanda finds a certain fascination with the sensitive perception shown in the poem. The subject of the poem, if she was real, must have left quite an impression on the poet. What he must have felt about her, and the way he chose to express it, weigh heavy with the mark of her presence. Yet those words say just as much about him.

Anger had crept into his words. He sensed a certain irresponsibility and weakness in her actions.

Amanda shivers. She is indeed intruding into the life of this man whom she knows only by his initials. V.M.

Up the road, a wisp of dust catches her eye. More than just a horse. A wagon must be heading this way. The dust cloud turns into the long path leading to the farm, and she realizes it's Wayne. He's returning much earlier than she'd anticipated.

She stuffs the paper into a pocket and quickly places the teak section of the box back in place, struggling to twist it the correct way. Finally it pops down. She then secures the sliding panel onto the top and closes the whole thing, wooden diamond sliding over and popping back into place. Amanda's eyes dart around. Where can she hide it? No time to run back to the barn. It's too large to slip under her clothes. Her eyes fall to the tall horse trough. The cloudy drink could hide it, yet she already values this silly box too much to plunge into the water.

Then she remembers where she found it. It was built to be waterproof, and it's already been in the ocean. She leans forward and dumps the box in with a splash.

It floats.

*Well, of course, it floats!* She finds a large rock, places it on top, and watches both box and rock settle to the bottom of the trough, out of sight.

Amanda grabs a nearby wooden bucket and lifts the handle of the pump. To Wayne, it will look like she's spent the sunny morning doing barnyard chores.

Her husband rides up, eyeing her. He remains silent for several moments, then plucks an extra-long toothpick from the corner of his mouth. She recognizes the little stick as the type they use to spear pickled hardboiled eggs from the big jar that sits on the end of Kelly's bar. Barely past breakfast and already he's been at it.

"And where did you go last night?"

"For a walk, Wayne. Just for a walk."

He looks like he wants to argue the point, but thinks the better of it. "Yeah, well, why aren't you inside now, tending to your preserves? That's what you said you'd be doing this week."

Amanda brushes a stray hair back from her forehead. "Because the chickens haven't been fed and the horse trough was near empty." She looks him in the eyes. "So I guess I'm doing my chores and some of yours too."

He squints at her. "Quiet, woman. If I want your fool comments, I'll ask you for 'em."

The horse steps forward and drinks heartily. It's probably the first time Wayne has offered the poor thing water since he left. She waits nervously until he points the horse toward the barn. Gazing down, she sees only murky water in the trough. There's no hint of what lurks below the surface.

# Chapter 12

## *To a Point*

Still fretting, Amanda heads back into the house. She will indeed tend to her preserves.

Wayne comes out of the barn with an ornery look. Out the window, she recognizes that look while he's still halfway across the yard. It's his cheap whiskey face. The drinks he consumed in the bar burn his stomach. Whiskey turns him into a lout. He knows how it affects him as well as she does, but when funds are tight, he drinks the cheap stuff anyway.

Wayne's pace quickens and she sees his determination. Amanda stands with her back to the door, calmly cutting the tops off plump strawberries, rinsing them in a bucket and throwing them in a pitted metal colander. She takes a deep breath and listens to the steady pat-pat-pat of water drops as they fall from the colander as it sits in the base of the yellowing porcelain sink.

Heavy boot steps in the back hall.

"And another thing!" he shouts, entering the kitchen, waving his finger like a bludgeon. "I do NOT like to hear that tone of voice out of you. Not ever. Do you understand?"

She remains cool. "What tone is that, Wayne?"

"You know what I'm saying! You're my wife, damn it, and you WILL respect me, do you under—" He realizes he is talking to the back of her head so he grasps her arm, spinning her around. His fingers continue clutching hard onto her arm to emphasize his point—squeezing hard enough to bruise.

She keeps the knife level as she turns, still holding a fat strawberry in her other hand. Their eyes meet. He drops his gaze down to the shiny blade.

"What's this?"

"What's what, Wayne?" She's not sure what she's doing. She feels ill, scared. But she holds her head high and doesn't move the hand that holds the knife.

"Are you threatening me with that?"

"I ... I don't think so, Wayne. I'm just cutting strawberries. Tending to my preserves." She stares him down. "How about you? Are you threatening me?"

A grinding sound comes from his teeth. He grabs at the base of the knife, but his inebriated swing lands his palm right on the blade instead. His tugs and ends up sliding his hand along the sharp edge. With a curse, he paws at the wound with his other had to stem the blood flow. Red drops fall to the dark wooden floor, making a *pat pat* sound that joins the sound of the water drops falling from the strawberries.

"Why you little heathen! You stabbed me!"

Shaking all over, Amanda manages to stand her ground. "I did no such thing, Wayne! You grabbed!"

"Don't give me that!" Another swing, this time at her face. She raises her hand to deflect it and ends up poking him again with the knife, dragging the blade down his wrist.

"Ow!" He steps backward. "Oh, you God damn bitch!" Fury in his eyes now, he swings both hands, flailing at her. There's an anger rising from him that goes beyond just this argument and this day. It holds months of his built-up resentment suddenly spilling out with no cork to contain it. It's aimed at her, at them, at the loneliness of the farm and the difference between their ages. It's anger at her lack of respect, and the gnawing frustration that he may not be worthy of respect.

Amanda knows he hates these feelings. But even more, he hates her for making him feel them.

She fends off each blow. Some get through, slapping at her head or hitting her shoulder. A hand-size red mark appears on her cheek. But she continues to defend herself, not even consciously cutting or sticking him as he swings. She just uses her right hand in a way she knows will protect her, and sometimes the knife helps slow his blows.

*He's gone mad this time. Totally mad.* She knew the anger was there, always lurking beneath the surface. But she hadn't expected it to come out so suddenly. She slowly backs toward the kitchen door. Finally Wayne stops, hugging his arms and bleeding from a good seven or eight wounds on his arms and hands. None are life-threatening. The first cut on his palm is still the worst of the slices.

"You stabbed me! You tried to kill me!"

"Wayne! I didn't! You know that."

"You witch! You did! I'll have the police on you!"

She shakes her head, spins and bolts and out the door, running full speed toward the barn. For once, Wayne's laziness pays off. He didn't bother to unsaddle Duncan, his quarter horse. The steed stands idly in the barn. With a single hop she jumps on a hay bale, places a leg against a support beam, and pulls herself up onto the saddle. As a city girl, she'd learned to ride horses belonging to her uncles and neighbors. Theirs was not the sort of neighborhood where she worried about riding like a proper lady. As a farm wife she'd tried to be more refined, usually riding in a proper wagon or sitting sidesaddle. But she still loved to ride her old way out in the fields. Early in their marriage Wayne used to ride with her, and he'd tease her about knowing how to ride like a man.

"I think the fact that I don't ride like a lady is one of the reasons you like me," she teased back.

Grabbing the reins, Amanda digs in her heels. Duncan quickly responds. She leans down and holds tight as he curves toward the barn door. They're at a full gallop by the time she passes the house. Wayne stands on the back porch, swearing and bleeding, cradling his arms like they're a couple of bright red newborn babies.

Hair loose and flowing behind her, she knows she must be a sight, dashing up the street at midday, horse hooves pounding. Unsure what to do, she makes her way two miles up the road to the house of Widow Ryan. She sees crisp, well-tended flower gardens and a white fence as she nears the home. The widow knows all too well what a woman like Amanda faces. She knows the old lady will help her.

But before she dismounts, Amanda thinks about what Wayne might do. If he sobers up, he might very well look for her here. The widow's house has been used before as a refuge for women who are upset with their husbands. Mrs. Ryan is known to be an outspoken suffragette.

She sits still in the saddle pondering her next move. Duncan occupies himself by munching grass and swatting flies with his tail.

She doesn't want to risk causing a scene at the home of this poor old woman. And she certainly doesn't want Wayne to catch up to her. What if he brings the police? If he gets to the authorities first and lies about what happened, they'll believe him. It does look like she stabbed him — more than once. She'll have no escape at all.

*What about other friends?* Yes, there are other places to which she could run. But word would get back to him, and it would travel quickly. She needs a clean break. She needs to go someplace where he'd never think of looking.

*But where?*

# Chapter 13

## *Spoils*

Glint of gold on a butterfly's trajectory.

Flipping end over end, a thick coin sails over the heads of pub patrons, toward the lightening-quick hand of a bartender who snatches it from the air. He stares at his catch and smiles. It's a twenty dollar Liberty Double Eagle—a rare sight in The Rose Point pub.

Across the room, Rudolph Baines, a recently wealthy diamond importer, holds up two fingers. The bartender nods and tugs at his beer tap. Baines smirks and returns to his conversation with a group of well-dressed businessmen. They all laugh about the expert flick of his fingers which sent the coin on its flight. They also whisper about how the pub owner greedily grabbed at the coin. Two or three of the group, slumming as they are this afternoon, exchange knowing glances.

Baines, who also speculates in real estate, has money to invest and each man at the table has deals to make with him. Why he brought them to this filthy pub for their negotiations is a mystery to them.

Baines looks toward a far corner of the room and sees faces prowling in the shadows. Several sets of eyes had watched the flight of the coin with quiet incredulity, and now they also see the laughter at the table. Something smolders back there, but Baines simply watches the watchers and smiles. As someone who wasn't wealthy at all in his youth, he feels a certain pride in their lurking envy.

Rarer even than a large gold coin are people foolish enough to flash them in the open. Only a stupid man, or a man very sure of his social status and his own protection, would conduct such a public display. The people in the corners of the pub seem to be evaluating Baines, trying to decide just what kind of man he is.

One face slowly emerges from the shadows. The man does not walk directly toward the table. Instead he stops near the bar, takes a drink, talks briefly to the bartender, then moves on.

He slowly moves closer. Listening. Eventually he stands close to Baines, who is not only ordering a full round of drinks for his table, but prodding one of the other men to share a story. The story, as it begins, provides a good excuse for others in the pub to draw closer. They lean in, listening. Soon there are over a dozen people seated or standing about the table.


The interior of The Rose Point Pub tends to grow dark long before the last of the sun's rays leave this spit of land that lies between the Charles and the Mystic Rivers. The place is known as Charlestown. The residents of Charlestown claim it's one of the oldest settlements in Boston, and this particular pub is one of the oldest in Charlestown.

No newfangled electric lights dangle here. No lantern oil either. It's cheap, fat-tallow candles for these tables. They spit and spark on the tables, adding a strange cooking scent to the cloud of tobacco smoke that always hovers near the ceiling.

Even when they're clean, the small windows at the front of The Rose Point, glass dimpled and bottom-thickened with age, do little to oblige the remaining sunlight. Where sun can penetrate, eyes can follow. The Rose Point remains careful about who it invites inside. Of those who do come in, some are sailors, some are workmen, and some are owners of businesses that don't have any official name. The manager of the pub, Johnson Aubrey, understands the needs of his customers, and makes the large room a place of subtle accommodation.

The haze and the poor lighting keep the corners dark. They are the types of corners that don't appreciate candles. Eyes slowly adjust, but details remain hidden.

It's just business.

There's also a tiny loft in the pub. Anyone looking down from above can see a huge round table near the center of the main floor. It can seat ten people around its perimeter and often plays host to afternoon card games. By late afternoon it serves as a central gathering place, where people drink and talk. Stranger may sit next to stranger. Nods turn to grunts. Occasionally the grunts turn to cautious talk and calculated friendship.

Baines has brought his four business associates here early in the afternoon. After their hushed talk and final nods, they move to the large table and begin chatting with others as the table fills up. As they learn a little about each man, they prod stories out of them.

The four well-dressed men at the center table have their reasons to be there. When speculating on land located near the waterfront, it's sometimes necessary to mix with the men who work there. It's the best way to learn who the stakeholders are and to know when change is looming. It's also a way to gain friends and influence through strong drinks and vague promises.

"What did you do then, Markley?" someone asks the man who has started to tell a story. It's a tale about his time with the railroad.

Markley is a stocky man in his late fifties. He's a pub regular, though a quiet one who mostly keeps to himself. He'd been reluctant to talk at first, but when he finally starts his story, the details come pouring out.

"Well, we shot every one of them damn buffalo that we could see. Honest to God, there must'a been six hundred of them. Took us about two hours, flanked 'em before they broke and that let us kept 'em running. Running right in a circle so as they wouldn't get away. Dumb animals couldn't even figure that out." Someone offers a low whistle.

"Not sure how many I got myself," Markley admits. "Figure it must have been over two dozen. Cleaned me right out of bullets. Others in my group got about the same, 'cept for one man who shot more than forty of 'em. We hired five skinners to come and help clean 'em up, and when they was finished, damned if those skulls weren't piled up high as a mountain. We all climbed on top to have our picture taken."

"That a fact?"

"Yes sir, it is. Sure as we're sittin' here."

"So how long was you in Kansas?"

"For working? Only about three months. Railroad sent me to Utah after then. But I'm telling you, that Sunday, when we all had the day off and about twenty-five of us went out together with our rifles, that was the best damn day of buffalo hunting I've ever seen. Best anyone in this country ever will see, I reckon."

"Weren't ya scared? So many of them running at you?"

"Can't say as I was. No time for it. Coming at us like a river, those damn beasts were. You should see their eyes. Anyone here ever hunt buffalo a 'for?"

A couple of the men smile and nod.

"Big, dark marbles. Like them Tronk steelies. Eyes so glassy you can't tell if they're looking at ya or not, ya know? They going to run at ya? Past ya? They don't seem to focus when they run. So you raise your gun, and you just shoot." His voice trails off for a moment as he takes another sip of beer.

"So anyways, we ate like kings for the rest of that week, I tell ya. Couldn't even give all the meat away, so we ate what we could and gave away what we could until it started to go bad. We gave over a ton of meat to two different railroad camps. Hell, we even gave another ton to an Indian village. The bastards cursed us, but they took it." Someone scoffs. Markley responds "Yeah, I know. But ya do what you can to keep the peace. Keep them Indians on our side if you can. That's what the railroad said. Next day some of them redskins even brought us back corn and beans and stuff. People said they don't like charity, so they wanted to treat the meat we gave them as trade. What the hell, fine with us. We ate the corn and gave a whole other bunch of beans and meat to a little town out there too. Don't know what the hell it was called."

Markley settles back in his chair with a satisfied grin. "Yes indeed. We all ate like kings that week. Goddamn hunter kings. That's what we was!"

The group murmurs its approval and envy.

As Markley finishes his story, Baines stays in firm control of the conversation. A few of the men start to tell their own hunting tales, but Baines cleverly steers the talk toward a pale man with a scar on his cheek and a bandage on his wrist. His rail-thin hand shakes as it grasps a glass mug. Baines orders the man another beer, prodding him to tell his own gritty tale.

"So I hear tell you were on that ship," Baines begins. "The one that sank a couple days ago out by the Banks. That a fact?"

The pale man looks at his fresh beer as it arrives. At first he too doesn't want to talk, but finally he takes a deep breath and looks around the circle. "Yeah. I was there, all right. Damn well wish I wasn't, but I was out there." He takes a long sip. "That's all I really want to say. Don't really like to think about it."

Some men at the table cast glances back and forth. Many of them are sailors and it's remarkable to them when they meet someone who's survived a serious shipwreck so far from shore. A survivor is blessed and cursed at the same time. In the superstitions of sailors, a shipwreck survivor has luck of some sort, and there's a feeling that it can rub off. Yet you're never quite sure if it's good luck or bad luck. Yes, they survived. But they experienced a good bit of the devil along the way, and their shipmates perished. He may have survived, but it wasn't very lucky for the other sailors, was it?

Still, sailors always gather near, at least on land. They feel an obligation to analyze a survival story when it's told, feeling the need learn its lessons.

"On the *Gossamer*? You were there?" one of the sailors asks.

Aubrey the barkeep lights a new candle and shoves its base down onto the soft sputtering wax of the old one. Before clearing the empty mugs, he offers Baines his change from the coin, but Baines waves it away.

"Yup. Just like I said." The survivor looks around the table. Several stone-hard faces look back at him. Maybe four or five more stand behind, waiting for his next word.

He shakes his head.

"I hear tell there was a demon on board. That the truth?"

The sailor closes his eyes. When no one talks, rumors and silly speculation rush in to fill the void. Others murmur. He decides that maybe it is time to tell more. The story is in there. It has to come out sometime.

"Okay then. Here it is. I was on the afternoon coal shovel, working with the fireman. Noon to four. That's my time and it's dusty duty. But it ain't all that bad if ya's in shape and you wears a kerchief over your mouth. So just after eight bells I had other cleaning duties, and then I was off duty until the late evening. So I was asleep in my bunk, waiting for chow, when things started to get bad."

Others at nearby tables stop to listen, turning around in their seats. News of the *Gossamer*, like any shipwreck, had made its way to ports up and down the coast. The loss of the *Gossamer* is particularly troublesome in Charlestown because of the ship's frequent Boston visits. The regulars at The Rose Point had known some of the sailors on board.

Devlin Richards is the man who emerged from the shadows several minutes before. He knows no one in this Yankee bar, and he's managed to say very few words in order to hide his Southern accent. He edges closer to Baines as the story unfolds. He doesn't particularly care about the story. His eyes aren't on the sailor, but on Baines. A few others notice the proximity, but say nothing. The Rose Point is the kind of place where you don't officially notice things.

"So how was it when the storm started? I mean … really?" Baines presses. His voice seems compassionate, but nervous eyes dart to the other listeners.

"What? Just before it went down?"

Nods all around the table.

"Funny thing. When it happened, all I was worried about was my life. Now that it's done, all I can think about is what I lost. I mean my own gear, you know? And friends. And some other stuff I wish I'd tried to save. But right then? It was only about me. And living."

"What do you mean, other stuff?"

"Well, you know how it is. There are holds and pockets and places on ships where the ships' officers fear to tread. Places harbormasters choose to ignore, fearful to climb down into the slime and brine that may lurk there. But for sailors who conquer this fear, places like that offer safe hiding and free passage for their own choice of freight. The tiny crawlspaces hold the most secret imports and exports of the docks, unloaded after hours and out of sight."

"Like what?" someone asks.

"Opium," someone says with a laugh.

"Bits of stolen gold."

"Aye," the sailor agrees. "Maybe ivory or amber too, or the pelts of exotic animals. As long as something can be wrapped tight and protected from the bilge rats and the slime that settles to the bottom of a ship, things like that are often worth the risk of smuggling. I ain't never been caught. I don't know any sailor who has. It's pretty damn easy."

The full-time sailors in the group nod in agreement. There are no manifests for the things sailors bring aboard. Small objects are quietly carried off in pockets and duffel bags. Larger items require a bit more creativity, but somehow they're removed too. Secret cargo is sold quietly into the shadow commerce that surrounds a port. Every harbor city in the world has places like The Rose Point. Local governments tend to tolerate them because they provide a service. As long as the vice is contained, pubs like this one can be as important to the local economy as any customs house. Police only crack down every few years to keep things from getting too out of control.

This afternoon the business of alcohol is brisk at the pub, but the business conducted in the shadows is not. The day's arrivals in Boston and Charlestown brought nothing more extravagant than a half case of absinthe from a Portuguese steamer and some cheap gold-plated stickpins via a French sailor. To everyone's surprise, an ancient English clipper that had visited The Philippines and then rounded South

America carried practically nothing—no opium and nary a stolen vase or a piece of jade in the lot. Most of that had been sold during a stop in Florida.

When business is slow, The Rose Point actually is at its most jovial. Conversations grow louder and the stories roll on. A man like Baines, orchestrating a conversation, looks only marginally suspicious. Devlin Richards, standing ever closer to Baines, doesn't look suspicious at all, unless one picks up on some special nuance.

The *Gossamer* survivor very much looks like a part of the story he tells. Terribly pale, his lifeless arm tucked to his side. A scar on his head has mostly healed, save its far reaches where the cut stubbornly refuses to close. He can see all the men at the table are listening. In other days he'd listened to such stores himself with a certain morbid fascination.

"Well, it was terrible. What else can I say?" He stares at the candle. Someone orders him a whiskey.

"Not just the storm, you know, but the way you see everything fall away beneath you. The ship, your mates, all that you've worked for, everything. Like your whole world is gone. All of it except for you. That's the strangest part. It's been your world, and then suddenly it forgets all about you and leaves you out there on your own."

He drinks the whiskey straight down. A shudder and an angry look show on his face.

"It didn't take long, really. The ship tipped on its side, then went down just like that. Sometimes they go bow up. Sometimes stern. But a ship that lays over on its side, and then eventually sinks perfectly level like that? Well, it's usually a good boat. Well-balanced and seaworthy. Nothing to blame really, just the luck of nature if a good ship gets knocked over or broke open."

Nods of agreement at the table. "Sometimes you don't know until a ship hits trouble just how good it is."

The survivor's voice drops to a whisper. The crowd leans forward, pressed tight around the table. Devlin Richards moves quietly with them and is now close enough to look into the breast pocket of Baines' coat. He sees nothing but a fine silk handkerchief. Below that, a watch chain is visible on the man's vest. Devlin stares at it, tongue pressed hard against the back of his teeth.

Standing on the other side of the table is a man who has often been seen around the docks in recent weeks. Like most of the others in the room, he wears work clothes. But his shirt and pants are neatly tailored and clean. Almost new. His fingernails are clean too. Neatly trimmed, just like his hair. He had been listening closely to Baines, but now he starts to study Devlin Richards and the way the man's eyes are drawn toward Baines' vest pocket. He says nothing, but shifts just enough so that he can keep a clear view.

"So tell us about the stuff you would have saved, if you had the chance." Baines seems to be looking for details about missing cargo, but the survivor isn't through yet with his tale of the wreck.

"I woke up when she started heeling," the sailor says, his good hand outstretched and rocking to show the motion. "Back and forth she went, over a bit more with each wave. I stayed in my bunk for most of it. Unless you're on duty, or an official storm station, you risk getting in the way. You also end up getting tossed around like a sack of flour, so it's best to just lay low."

He looks Baines in the eyes. "Comes a time when the sound changes though, you know?" His eyes travel on to meet the eyes of the other sailors around the table. "Time when the waves break, and you know they's all getting far too tall and too dangerous. That was the toughest time for me. Just the waiting and wondering. Couldn't wait anymore."

"How many were there on board?" This time the question comes from the workman with the clean clothes and neat hair. He's stopped studying Devlin for the moment. Suspicious looks around the table hint that they barely recognize him. Even if they didn't know him, they know his type. Probably knows a little about dock work and a lot about places like The Rose Point. Such men tend to arrive and depart quickly. Political baggage in tow. Labor trouble in their wake.

The sailor looks up. "There was twenty-seven of us. Well, twenty-eight actually—crew and one extra passenger."

The man nods and asks, "One extra?"

"Aye. Scientist of some type. Had a couple of crates of equipment with him. Doing some kind of test before we headed on to England. We all thought it was a waste of our time—just wanted to get where we was headed with no delays. But he paid for the time and trouble."

"What was he doing?"

"Never did find out. He never got to fully unpack them crates."

"How many survivors?"

"Just me and the cook."

Baines interrupts, pulling the conversation back on track. His track. "So the ship, she just tipped over?"

"Slammed over. She was fight'n it pretty good at first. Riding up and down like a damn cork. Like I said, good ship. But we started getting slapped instead of bobbing. Only a matter of time if they crest big and stay big like that. You all know it. You're just waiting for one that comes in at an odd angle and catches you broadside and tears at ya."

"That what happened?"

The survivor glowers. "Ain't it just what always happens? Think back to your storm stories, boy. Back to your youth when you sat around listening to men like me telling stories just like mine. Stories always been the same, ain't they? The crew fights. They keep bow to the waves, but there's always one waiting out there and it slams ya. If you're good like a cork, ya tip and then you slowly make right again. But once the water gets in, it slows you like a bloated fish. You come up so slow that you're not ready for the next ones, and the ones after that. They do their foul deed on ya. Like hell's suddenly grabbed you by your jewels. That's what happened to us. Lost some ports. Lost a hatch just like God scraped it off with a razor. Water came in, and we were done."

Some nod. Some look at their beers.

"When things got that bad, I came off my bunk faster than the devil. I put on my raincoat and boots and headed toward the engine room. Nothing I could do, but I had to do something. I had to be out there, fighting it along with them.

I climbed up to the mid deck. Never got to the engine room though. I was in the main companionway when we went over. I think that's why I made it. Hatch came off right above me and suddenly I was tumbling into a waterfall. Coldest damn water I've ever felt. Slammed me around once, twice. I'm not really sure. … Found myself floating, and I could see right out the hatch, so's I just swam on through it, out into the open water. The cook was already on the surface, clinging to some boards. The damn fool had been out on the deck, he said. On his way to the wheelhouse to ask the captain if he should cancel the evening meal. Funny how being stupid is what got him outside, and saved his damn life."

He squints at the faces. Baines starts to interrupt, but the sailor holds up a finger.

"The strangest thing was the way she sank on her side, then stayed there for a bit, maybe thirty feet down. You could see her lurking down there. Creepy as a damn ghost. Thousands of tiny bubbles coming up. Just hovered like she had second thoughts, like maybe she wanted to come back up. The cook and I were clinging to some boxes and looking down. But the waves kept bouncing her, and with each rise and fall, she burped out more bubbles. She was just rocking and waiting to die. Then there was this terrible groan. Like she was crumpling up. That's all I saw really. We were swept away, puking and swearing and praying that it would be over. Kept looking back, both of us, to see if anyone else came up, dead or alive, but there was no one else. The waves were up and down all night, and we kept looking, and eating foam and hanging onto those planks until the next day."

He looks around once more at all the eyes. He sees blank looks and drawn faces. It could have been any one of them.

"I had no strength left. None. Just locked my hands around some loose boards. I figured I'd be found that way someday. My death grip. But a fishing boat on its way back from the Banks spotted us right after the storm passed. Said they saw lots of wreckage and they just started following it and prowling around to see if there were survivors. They hauled us aboard. We was in the water maybe eighteen hours. I was as goddamn cold as I've ever been."

He draws a series of circles on the tabletop.

"Even though we told them there weren't no others, they sailed in circles, like this, for another day, still looking and hoping. Guess the cook and I was hoping too. But there was no one else—just trash bobbing around on an empty sea."

Devlin Richards watches as Robert Baines pushes slightly away from the table. The rich man reaches into his coat and pats his inside pocket. Devlin finishes his own beer and wipes his lips on his sleeve.

"So I wonder what was in those crates of his," the man in the clean work clothes muses.

The sailor studies him. "Where are you from, stranger?"

"Me? Why, I came up from Mystic just yesterday. My name's Jeb." He extends a hand. "Jeb Thomas." The sailor regards him coolly and doesn't shake his hand.

"I don't much care what was in the crates. Far as I'm concerned, they were cursed. He was cursed too. Kept us out there just a little too long. Trying to mess with nature, that's what I saw. We would've been well east of the storm if we hadn't lingered."

"What do you mean, 'mess with nature'?"

"Well, he said he could maybe help ships talk to each other from hundreds of miles apart. It's like he was practicing some kind of electric voodoo. It ain't natural, and I say the devil took him for that. Devil took a lot of my friends along with him. So you ask me what was in them crates? Voodoo tools. And now I'm glad them crates are on the bottom. I'm glad I'm not there with 'em, and I'm damn glad he's gone."

Jeb presses on. "Were the crates down below?"

"No. He stored 'em topside."

"So this scientist … was he from around here?"

"Yeah, said he was local. He talked a good bit to others on the crew. Said he had a place down by the rail yards. Had the back rooms of that big brown warehouse you can see just beyond the tracks. Lived there and had some sort of lab."

Jeb nods.

Baines interrupts, eyeing this man Jeb suspiciously. "Did you see his crates in the wreckage at all? Did they float free?"

"Don't know. Don't care. The hell with them."

"And if you had to guess?"

"If I had to guess, I'd say they broke off and floated away. They was topside after all. They was lashed down, but the way the *Gossamer* was pitching, and the way the waves were hitting, I'd guess they was washed away before she went down."

Baines rises. "I want to thank you, kind sir, for sharing the story with us. It was most enlightening, and, I'm sure, not much fun to remember. God bless you, sir, for what you've been through. And God bless those other poor souls too."

The sailor nods and shakes Baines' hand. "God has a special place for sailors," says the sailor. "I know he does. Fair skies and following seas. That's what you find in God's good heaven." He looks toward the window, holding his limp arm and lost in remembrance.

"Yes indeed," Baines replies as he pulls on his dark cap and heads for the door. It's a heavy oak plank with iron strap-style hinges that reach across the width of the door. His friends go with him, and they gather outside the door for a brief chat.

Devlin Richards waits a few discreet moments and follows, head down, hands in his pockets. Outside, he pulls his scarf up and his hat down. It's finally grown dark. He walks past the group and into the inky night.

# Chapter 14

## *Away*

A road leads to the east. As she sits atop Duncan, Amanda's eye is drawn to its vanishing point. She knows where the road goes. She's traveled its length before. But now it calls to her in a different way. Her last trip in that direction was a good one. It's in the general direction of where she reached the wreckage from the *Gossamer*, though this road will curve away, toward a different place.

If she were to ride up this road a couple of miles, she might be able to find that nice old couple who gave her a ride in their strange steam wagon.

When she had finished walking the shore and sculching the wreckage, the couple had offered her a ride back to the road. They were a delightful pair. They told her where they lived and to come visit anytime. They seemed to be good people. Perhaps they'd understand.

Hesitantly she tugs on the reins. The horse is unconvinced that Amanda really wants to go, so he circles quickly. She hangs on tightly as Duncan returns to the tasty grass, lowering his head so quickly that she's suddenly pulled forward, hanging onto his neck. The unexpected transfer of weight makes the horse stumble, and he snorts in pain.

As he regains his stance, Amanda pulls herself back to the center of the saddle. The horse walks toward a patch of shady clover, and she can feel him favoring his front right hoof. He lifts it, then sets it down tentatively, slowly trying to transfer some weight onto it.

A lame horse could greatly complicate her escape. She leans forward, to whisper in its ear.

"Come on, Duncan. I need your help, boy. Can you do it? Can you help me?"

She strokes his thick neck. Urges him onward.

As with most of the animals on the farm, Amanda is the one who feeds Duncan. He gets extra apples and sugar from her, and they have a solid bond. He gives her a bit of a grunt, then starts walking, a slight limp in his gait. As they head up the road, she doesn't dare push him to a trot. Instead she looks nervously over her shoulder.

Eventually she nears a farmhouse. Based on their description, she believes it's theirs. "Quincy, that was their last name," she mumbles to herself. Wayne knows nothing of these people, just as he knows nothing of her visit to the shore. She never got around to telling him where she had been nor showing him the compass.

As she approaches the fields near their house, she takes the measure of Duncan again and decides his foot is surviving the trip. She spies a figure in a light yellow dress in the side yard, heading for the house. That must be Agnes.

Her nervousness about what may lurk behind finally gets the better of her. "Ha-ya!" she cries, yanking the reins. "Up! Get 'er up!" And Duncan does, heading down the road at a trot, rising to a full gallop as she flicks the reins side to side, steering them into the pasture. She loves the feel of the horse beneath her. He's pushing himself. He's dealing with the pain in his foot. He's taking her out of harm's way, into the safety of this home. Hooves beat thunder over the open field, echoing in tight as she passes a small stand of trees.

Reaching the side of the yard, she can feel Duncan limping more. She slows, patting his neck, a bit angry at herself for making him work so hard, but proud of him for doing it. They limp onward. Her face is dirty and her skirts wrinkled from time in the saddle.

Agnes Quincy hurries over to meet her, giving her a solid farm-woman hug.

"Goodness, I didn't expect to see you again so soon, dear!"

"I didn't expect to be here," she admits.

Agnes can sense that Amanda's in trouble. The two whisper to each other as Duncan limps off toward the backyard, looking for clover, water, and shade. Once Agnes understands what's happening, Amanda is taken in, like a stray kitten in need of a meal.

"We have soup on the stove, dear, and fresh bread. I don't have any butter yet. That's this afternoon's chore. But …," she looks toward her kitchen, "let's see what else we can find."

Famished, Amanda sucks down the soup, some leftover baked beans, and a wonderful yellowish bread that steams from its center as she breaks it open. It smells amazing and tastes like cornmeal mixed with some other grains—a typical end-of-the-week concoction that farm wives are so good at throwing together.

All through the meal Amanda apologizes for the urgency in her arrival. "I just … I didn't know where else to turn. He'll look for me at all of our friends' houses. He doesn't know you at all. So I thought … well … I'm sorry."

"Nonsense!" Agnes pats her hand. "Now don't you even mention it, dear. You've had a tough time these past few days, and we're happy to help."

Agnes gives a long sideways glance at her husband, who's just risen from his nap. He wears brown workpants and the top to a set of gray long johns. Thick suspenders are off his shoulders and hanging to his knees. Amanda senses both love and worry in Agnes' gaze.

When Amanda first met the couple, she'd thought that Elmer was rather pale and thin. Looking at him now, the word "gaunt" comes to mind instead. His skin looks bluish white. His breathing is shallow. As he notices Amanda looking, he smiles, fixes his suspenders, clears his throat, and whispers in a gravelly voice.

"Well then, what have we here? Hello again, young lady!"

"Hello Mr. Quincy," she smiles.

"Young Amanda is paying us a visit, dear," says Agnes. "But I fear it's not for a good reason. She's in a bit of trouble."

"Is that so?" He dishes himself a painfully small cup of soup and grabs a tiny chunk of bread before he joins them at the green wooden table. "Well, we're glad you came here. Glad we can help. You seem like a fine girl." He dunks the bread and nibbles at it, looking first at his wife, and then at Amanda. "So what seems to be the trouble?"

Agnes quickly brings him up to speed on Amanda's escape, and her decision to seek refuge with them instead of staying closer to home.

"She's expressed an interest in possibly returning to Boston, Elmer. I'm sure we can help her get to a train or something."

For the first time, Amanda looks closely at Elmer, and she has a suspicion why he looks so ill. It's a look she's seen before. It's probably cancer. The old man has the identical look of a neighbor of hers who died from a bad cancer a few years before she left Boston.

At least everyone assumed it was cancer. Hushed whispers around the parlor during his wake raised suspicions but never quite confirmed it. Polite company never seemed to want to discuss the dreaded disease. Just saying the word seemed to carry some risk. A curse. A death sentence best left to whispers.

Amanda glances along the kitchen counter until her eyes come to rest on a dark brown bottle with a glass stopper. The stopper is barely pushed into the neck of the bottle, as if Elmer lacks the energy to press it harder. She immediately recognizes the container. It's morphine. Swig as needed for pain and the doctor will always leave another bottle when he visits. It's the only escape, short of death, that a cancer patient can find.

Amanda stammers, "I ... I'm interrupting. You're not well. You don't need me here complicating things. I should ..."

"Nonsense child," Agnes assures her. "This old farm doesn't have enough visitors. If it wasn't for the pastor who comes out once a week, and occasionally our neighbor Carl, why, I don't think we'd see another soul from one month to the next."

Amanda leans back, looking at both of them. "But you're ...," she nods directly to Elmer, "I mean, I'm sure you barely have the energy to sit here with us right now."

He leans forward, eyes locked on to hers, clearing his throat with the conviction of a politician about to make a speech.

"You're very astute, young lady. I am not doing well at all. I'm sure you could tell that back when we were at the shore. I mostly sat in the wagon." He lets out a low cough, then clears his throat. "But my wife also is correct when she says you are not intruding. I hope you will listen to her. Just having someone around, especially someone with your youth and energy, is enough to brighten up this room. Let me tell you, dear, we really need to have these rooms brightened a bit."

"Well, yes. I could ... I mean, I do want to stay. But ... I should sleep in the barn," she continues, "and be on my way in the morning."

"You will certainly not sleep in the barn," Agnes insists. "You'll sleep in our spare room, and have breakfast with us in the morning. And you'll stay as long as you like, you hear?"

With a slight tilt of her head, Amanda sits, considering. These are kind people. Kind to her on the road, kind on the way back from the beach, and kind to her now, – here in their home. It restores her faith in how nice people can be. And the love they show toward each other also shows her how a man can treat a woman, at least when he's a good man.

"I do thank you then. It's very gracious of you."

They spend the rest of the afternoon sitting near the fire, even though the day is far from cold. Agnes serves tea. It's been years since Amanda has seen such a lovely teapot. It's blue and white, with painted flowers on the side and a rim of bright gold. Agnes handles it expertly, her spotted hands pouring and lifting, with a slight bounce, at just the right moment. She doesn't spill a drop. They can tell that Amanda is distressed by her situation, so Elmer starts to tell Amanda a meandering but strangely interesting story about his brother, a fellow veteran of the Union Army. The brother was wounded at Harpers Ferry.

"We all thought he was done. Apparently he was under a tree that was cut in two by a cannonball. A huge branch fell, landing on him and knocking him out. He also got pieces of the shattered cannonball in his shoulder. Dang thing split into pieces when it hit the tree. Rebels didn't always have the best quality armaments. Anyway his fellow soldiers found him right quick and pulled the branch off him, but he was unconscious for days. I managed to get leave—I was in Virginia at the time—and went to see him. Said my good-byes, I did. Stood right at his bedside. Never expected to see him awake again."

Elmer leans forward. "But I did see him. We all did. Here it is, more than twenty-five years later, and my brother is still around. Not the same as he once was, mind you. Limps like hell. Slurs his words now and then when he's tired. But he's alive and well. Wasn't even married when he was wounded, but he met a nice girl and he went on to be the father of four and grandfather of one so far."

He looks at Amanda. "Back twenty-five years ago I never dreamt that he'd outlive me. Not with all that damage he had. But he's still going strong and I'm winding down. A body never really knows what's going to happen. Do they?"

She smiles slightly. "No sir. I guess they don't."

"Just like you didn't know what you were getting into when you got married. Things just happen ... things that are out of your control."

She looks at him, then looks down at the floor.

"That's all I really have to say about it. Things happen. You make your guesses about what life might bring you. You make your plans, but you never really know what you're getting into. It's half chance. You can't feel bad about your choices when you guess wrong. At least you took a shot at it." He smiles at her. "I know how women like to talk. Men too. But no matter what the women at your parish might say, you did what you could do, dear. It's not your fault if things failed."

They drink more of the tea, then Amanda helps Agnes clear the table.

"Will you be okay?" she asks the old woman when they're alone. "I mean, after he's gone?"

Agnes nods, but stares into the sink as she places a glass in a soapy metal pan. "Yes, I'll be all right. Financially anyway. We received a bit of money from an uncle of Elmer's a while back, so at least the farm is paid off. Got a little in the bank too."

"Is that the same uncle who gave you that steam wagon?"

Agnes laughs. "That cursed thing? Yes. And I've always hated it. Scares me to death, going that fast, and all the noise

127

and the sparks." She shakes her head. "It isn't much more than a toy for Elmer anyway. He only drives it on special occasions. I'll be happy to never ride in it again."

She scrubs a clear glass, holds it to the light, and then hands it to Amanda, who plunges it into a pot of hot rinse water. They repeat the process for each of the dishes, then use the dirty water to wash the sooty tops of the kerosene lamps.

They talk more about Elmer's long-since deceased uncle. He owned some kind of machine shop and made a good bit of money during the war. He had no children of his own, so he spent his money on silly contraptions like that wagon. "He left a little something to all of his nieces and nephews when he died. Elmer got the wagon. I would have preferred a good plow horse."

"Where did it come from?"

"I'm not sure. But it's a lot older than you think. You probably know it's not much like the new automobiles that you hear about. Elmer thinks it was built for use by the Union Army during the war. They hauled equipment by train, but the train tracks didn't usually reach to the frontlines. The wagon was sort of a small locomotive built so that it didn't need a track. It has basic steering, and they could swap out different kinds of wheels depending on the terrain. He doesn't think it got much use during the war though. Turned out to be too temperamental."

Amanda nods. "The day it carried us to the beach, Mr. Quincy said he'd made some repairs on it."

"Oh yes, he's tinkered with the foul thing a good long time. Even towed it to a blacksmith once. The silly tank had rusted out, but they patched it and cleaned it all out. Elmer worked for the railroad back in the seventies, so he knows a good bit about steam power and how it all works."

Amanda collects the clean lamp chimneys and dries them, switching from a towel to the bottom of her apron when the towel becomes too wet.

"So, dear, enough about my future without Elmer. What will you do for the long term? Do you think you'll leave him for good?"

"I don't know. I have to leave for now anyway. I just need to figure out where to go."

Agnes places a hand on the young woman's shoulder. "Well, it's a hard decision, but not a bad one I'd say. Still, you know what will happen. A separated woman. Or divorced, if you manage to obtain a divorce. Well, the world won't always look kindly on you, dear."

"I know." Amanda thinks for a moment. "I don't even know how to get a divorce. I've never looked into it."

"Well, I think the law will only give you one if you can prove adultery, long absence, or cruelty. Sounds to me like you might qualify for the later. But if he fights it, it can be pretty tough to prove."

Amanda nods. "Not very fair, is it?"

"No dear. It's not fair at all. But then, the laws weren't written by women, were they?"

"I might be better off just disappearing. Going somewhere and starting over and not even worrying about what I've left behind here."

Agnes pours out the dishwater and wipes her hands. She pulls off her apron and hangs it on a nail beside the sink. But she holds onto the material for a moment, studying the faded checkered pattern. "He gave me this. Ten years ago at least. Silly present, don't you think? Not very romantic. But still." She blinks several times.

"Do you have family in the area?"

"Yes," Agnes nods. "And so does he. A few miles away. Believe me, that's a godsend now that he's sick. His sisters and nephews have been a real help around here." She smiles at Amanda. "How about you, dear?"

"Family? No. No one on the Cape. Not anywhere around here really. My mother died two years ago. I have a brother who settled in Chicago. We've fallen out of touch. I might still have a cousin in Boston, but I don't know how to make contact." She can see the worry in Agnes' eyes.

"Listen, I do have old friends in Boston. I just need to get there. I can take the train. Duncan is too lame to make the trip."

"Now now, you can stay here if you need to, dear. Lord knows I could use the company."

Amanda shakes her head. "No, you have your own problems right now. And I need to make myself scarce. I would like to come back and visit though. Sometime. Maybe in the fall."

Agnes smiles. "I'd like that, very much."

They return to the parlor to find Elmer asleep on the davenport. His wife covers him with her shawl, kissing his forehead. Amanda feels a pang of jealousy for what they share. Despite the looming end, she sees a kind and gentle love that she and Wayne were never able to build. But she would have shared such a love with him, if he had allowed it. Amanda so longed to build that trust and intimacy. But he was content with a few grunts of alleged intimacy, followed by sleep.

Ostensible lover by night and a stranger by day.

Before bed, Amanda leads Duncan into the barn. Finding an empty stall, she waters him, gives him fresh hay and carrots. She rubs some liniment on his leg and strokes his nose until her own legs grow tired.

That night she sleeps restlessly in the Quincys' spare bedroom. Her path seems so uncertain. She lacks even the train fare for her escape trip to Boston. With some dread, she knows she must somehow get back to her house, to sneak in and retrieve some money and the silverware that she claimed on the beach. It's risky, but it's the only way she'll survive.

She rises with the sun and finds Agnes and Elmer already awake. Elmer limps in the back door, brushing oats off his faded blue work jacket. It's good to see him up and about, Amanda remarks.

"Good days and bad, my dear. You've seen me at my worst and now my best, such as it is."

He jerks his thumb back toward the barn. "That horse of yours isn't going anywhere."

She nods.

"He's got a lame leg. Front right."

"I know."

"It's good and swollen. He needs to sit tight for a few days."

"But I … need to get back to my house!"

Agnes' eyes widen. "Whatever for, child?"

"I think you know. I need to get what's mine. I need …," her voice trails off.

"You need money. Things of value so that you can leave."

She nods.

Agnes walks toward her. "Because they could be your ticket out?"

"Yes."

"I understand."

"Thank you. But now I don't know what to do if Duncan can't make it at least that far."

"It's very dangerous for you to go back there, you know. You're foolish to try. What if he catches you? What if he has you arrested?"

"I'm not worried. These days he goes into town to drink almost every afternoon. He mostly goes to Kelly's or to The Orleans Inn."

Elmer laughs. "Snow's Folly? You know that place was built with cargo claimed from a wrecked schooner, don't you? Wrecked right on the same beach where we met you, I believe."

Amanda nods. "Yes, I know. Wayne told me the story."

"Look, dear, if you decide to go home while he's out, I'm definitely going with you."

"Nonsense, Mrs. Quincy. I couldn't. I won't put you in danger. I have to do this alone."

"You're right. You won't put me in danger because we're going to do it tomorrow, and we're going to do it like this." She starts to move things around on the table. "We'll do it so that you don't get caught."

"Give me a rough idea of the layout of your farm and where it's located."

Agnes arranges glasses and salt shakers, mapping out a route back to the farm. After a few minutes of discussion, she offers some ideas.

"You see? If we hide here and wait for him to leave, then we can see all the way to here, and we could slip through here ...."

Amanda points and talks and moves the items around. Slowly, a raiding plan begins to take shape.

# Chapter 15

## *The Mark*

The first time Devlin Richards tries to follow Rudolf Baines he doesn't have much luck. Baines stays with his group as they leave the pub. Devlin ends up walking with them for a time, making small talk and hoping that the group breaks up. That doesn't happen. They stick together until Devlin realizes he risks wearing out his welcome.

The group returns the next night, again talking to sailors and gathering information about the wreck of the *Gossamer*. They also talk about the comings and goings of ships at the local piers.

Again Devlin follows the group as they head outside. When the men see him, their voices drop. He lingers several feet away, lighting a cigarette and pretending he's having trouble with the match.

"So what do you think?" one of Baines group whispers to the others. Devlin realizes they're again talking about the shipwreck of a few nights ago.

"I'm interested in learning more about those big crates. The ones with his test equipment. I think it's possible that they floated free, but what are the chances of ever finding them?"

"They say the wreckage came ashore on the eastern edge of Cape Cod," says a man in a brown bowler hat.

"Yes, but they probably broke apart before then, and whatever was left was hauled away by some scavenger. No one down there is about to tell us what they found."

"So you don't think it's worth looking?"

"I don't know. Worth making some inquiries, I guess. If we ever find his stuff, maybe we can buy it. I know some people we can hire to figure it out."

"But what's stuff like that really worth? Even if we could find it, how much could we sell it for and what's the market?"

"I know, I know. But think about it. Isn't it worth a little gamble?"

Baines quiets the group with a final comment. "I'll telegraph an attorney friend down there and have him ask a few questions. We'll at least get an idea of what was found. We'll go from there."


Devlin walks about 400 feet ahead of the group, then slips into a stand of trees. If his guess is correct, Baines will return to Boston this evening, and there's only one way he can go.

Baines isn't riding a horse. Devlin watches him say good-bye to his friends. He then walks up the street. Surprisingly, he zigzags up a few blocks, as if to see if anyone is following, then heads toward the narrows that lead into Boston. In a few hundred yards he enters a stretch of a quiet street, and Devlin hurries his pace and walks behind him.

"You there!" Devlin calls out.

Baines turns, hand entering the right pocket of his oversize coat. Distrust in his eyes.

Devlin Richards soothes with his voice. "Hey, thanks for getting that sailor to talk yesterday. I had been wondering what happened on the *Gossamer*. Sad thing that ...."

Baines nods, unimpressed. "You again! And what brings you out here tonight, sir?"

"Just heading home." He does his best to mimic a Boston accent. "Looks like we're headed the same way, friend. Not always safe around here. Better to walk in groups."

To appear less threatening, he walks past Baines and continues up the sidewalk, like he's continuing his journey. Gazing back over his shoulder, he says, "Your choice, of course."

Baines relaxes a bit. "Where you heading?"

"I have a friend who lives but a few blocks from Faneuil Hall. We agreed to meet tonight, but I can never catch a cab on this side of the river. I shouldn't have lingered so long at The Rose. But it's always interesting, what's happening there, eh?"

Baines nods. There's an uneasy silence as they press onward.

"You travel overseas yourself?" Devlin asks. They're walking side by side now across the narrowing causeway.

"Maybe once a year. I'm in the import business, but I prefer to work mostly from this end. Family and all. That makes it hard to be away for months at a time."

Devlin watches quietly out of the corner of his eye. Baines seems to be about his same height. A little older, but fit from walking. Devlin could probably take him. But that pocket, large enough for a revolver, worries him.

"So what sort of things do you import?"

"Rugs," Baines says. "Some from China. I can't tolerate the damage though. Seems everything I get from there gets soaked along the way. They're not much for packing things up the right way."

Devlin wonders about this. He had heard Baines was a jeweler, not a rug merchant. "Oriental too?"

"Meaning Persia? Yes, usually via Cape Town, believe it or not. My man there finds what he needs coming in on the local steamers that ply the East African Coast. It's cheaper to ship cargo out of Africa than from Persia. That's my business trick. Same rugs, different point of departure for some decent savings."

Devlin Richards' eye widen. That would explain a lot. If he does business through South Africa, he could also be in the diamond business. This was a good pick for him—a merchant who deals in diamonds and rugs. A merchant who carries mostly coins. He hasn't felt this much anticipation about a mark in years. As they enter a dark empty street, Devlin realizes it's the best time to make his move. It has to be a surprise, given the possibility of a weapon.

"Hold on," Devlin says, stooping to tie the lace on his shoe. Once kneeling, he tugs at the laces, but he also slips a long knife from a sheath tied to his ankle. Darkness covers his movements.

"Never been to Africa," he says as he stands.

"Hell of a place," Baines grunts as they turn to walk on. "Some of the people are wonderful. So friendly—smiling and laughing with you. Then you'll turn around and see such ugliness. Leprosy. Slave trading. They say it doesn't exist

137

anymore, but oh, let me tell you, the slave trade is still there. Such terrible people."

Devlin grits his teeth in anger.

"You can see it all in the Dark Continent. It's a strange and wonderful land."

With Baines a step ahead of him, Devlin has a clear shot. He raises his arm and brings the knife down hard, aiming for a space between Baines' shoulder blades. The thrust is true and hard.

# Chapter 16

## *Not Quietly*


But because Baines is walking, or maybe because his coat is too thick, the knife doesn't plunge deep enough for an instant kill. It goes in maybe two inches, and no further. The older man groans and gasps, falling forward.

Richards yanks the knife back out and drops to his knees beside his victim, who's lying face-down. Blood spills onto the walkway near the man's collar as Devlin raises the knife again.

"You bastard!" Baines spits. "I should have known."

He squirms onto his side. "And I did know. I could see it in you! What a fool I was!" He tugs at his pocket. Finding the opening, he thrusts his hand in and doesn't bother to pull out the gun. He finds the trigger and rolls slightly, trying to point the barrel up toward his attacker.

The gun makes a muffled pop as Richards brings the blade down again. Something hot grazes his thigh. The blast makes Devlin jump just enough to miss. The knife strikes the stones of the street with a sickening clank. Baines continues to twist away.

Panicked now, Devlin is concerned that the gunshot, even though muffled, will bring people to the street. He shifts his weight and brings his knee down directly on Baines' coat pocket, forcing the gun hand to the side and away from him. He can feel the hand struggling to lift the gun and fire another round. Quickly, with practiced skill, Devlin thrusts the knife into Baines' sternum and twists it upwards. The man's eyes widen. The gun fires again, but in a random direction. In a moment, the struggling stops.

Eyes scanning the street. No one saw anything, did they? Not in this darkness. His hands work fast, finding pocket after pocket, collecting all he can. The vest holds the coveted watch and chain. The inside coat pocket holds five more gold coins. Devlin can't tell their exact value in the dark, but at least two of them feel quite hefty. He also grabs a stick pin from Baines' tie before turning the body over. There's a thin leather fold in the back pocket, maybe five bills inside. One of them is a twenty.

Kicking the body back over, he checks for gold teeth and finds only one. It's way in the back and he decides to leave it, rather than spending several precious moments trying to pry it out. It's a shame that there's blood on the coat. It might have fit him.

Hat and scarf back in place, Richards crams the stolen goods into his own pockets and steps over the body. He looks in all directions as he walks. No one in sight. He walks quickly. After two blocks, he starts to relax. Only then does he feel a trickle of blood along his leg. He touches the wound where the bullet grazed his leg and decides it's not bad. But there's enough blood on his leg that it's visible. He needs to get off the street.

*It wasn't enough.*

Devlin can tell by the feel of the loot in his pocket. It's a start, but the whole take won't add up to even one hundred dollars. It won't fill his bag and leave him satisfied enough for his trip back south. He needs more. Much more.

More time. More money. He'll return to The Rose Point. Clayton Harkins was right about the place. It's a good place to sit and watch. He needs another ship to come in. Another deal. He needs to be more than just a damned street thief.

As Devlin walks, he starts to wonder about that scientist the sailor mentioned, the one who did his experiments on the *Gossamer*. He mentioned his name at some point. Victor something. If what that fool sailor said was true, then the man's apartment probably isn't far away. And since he died recently, it probably hasn't been cleaned out yet. He might be able to find it, especially since he knows the warehouse that was mentioned.

He turns around and heads back in the direction of Charlestown. He doesn't know a single person who might buy stolen scientific equipment, but if he can find one, raiding the apartment and lab might give him another good score.

What he doesn't see is a man lurking in a space between two houses, watching his every move.

# Chapter 17

## *Return*

"It's a foolish stunt," Elmer Quincy tells the women when he discovers what they're plotting. "You'll get yourself hurt. Or maybe arrested. And how are we going to explain that to the neighbors?"

But Amanda is determined to return to the barn to claim what's hers. Agnes is supportive, even giddy, at the idea of helping. Instead of fighting it, Elmer realizes that he needs to help them with their planning. He talks direction and strategy, shaking his head now and then at the brashness of it all.

Two mornings later Amanda and Agnes rise before dawn. They choose to stay away from the steam wagon and instead hitch the family buckboard to two sturdy horses, a large chestnut bay and a slightly smaller brown Morgan. It's still dark when they head back to Amanda's place. Her "ex-home" she calls it now. Their goal is to avoid Wayne while gathering what's hers.

At Amanda's direction, Agnes pulls the wagon onto a narrow farm trail about a mile from the Malcolm farm. The trail stretches through a woods and around the back of the property. They should be able to draw within 200 yards of the house without being seen. As they near the edge of the woods, they stop the wagon and wait for a moment, listening.

Hearing nothing, save the fussing and calling of predawn birds, Amanda climbs down from the wagon and walks, crouched low, toward the clearing. She can see a light in the window of their bedroom. Inside, past the sheer curtain, she can see Wayne's silhouette as he pulls on a work shirt. If his routine is typical, he'll sit to tie his boots then head to the kitchen for toast, an apple, and some bacon.

It's a Saturday. She and Agnes specifically chose this morning because there's a small farmers' market downtown. Wayne heads out early on market days. He'll bring fruit from the trees near the house, or sometimes he'll carry a crate of chickens if they have a healthy new batch of chicks to replace them. Market days are good quick money. Sometimes Wayne brought the profits home and sometimes he took them to a pub. But anytime he heads out on market day with things to sell, Amanda knows Wayne will be gone for several hours.

A match is struck in the kitchen, and a small lamp is lit. As the light comes up, she smiles to see several brown crates sitting on the kitchen table. It's not like him to think so far ahead, but it looks like he packed up the fruit the night before. At least she and Agnes won't have to wait while he visits the trees to pick the fruit.

Agnes appears at her side. "Get down. He's coming out!" They crouch low and stare at the door as Wayne steps outside.

Amanda's eyes widen. The crates don't contain fruit at all. It looks like they're full of glass jars with thick waxy tops. It's her fruit preserves, and by the number of crates, it looks like he's emptied her entire stock. Is that what he's planning to sell at the market? She starts to stand, as if she plans to yell at him, but Agnes tugs her down.

"What are you doing?"

"Those are my preserves!" she whispers loudly. "What does he think he's doing?"

"It doesn't matter, dear. It's not like you're going to take them with you!"

"Well, no. But he doesn't know that! I mean ...." She swallows hard. She's not sure if this action represents his acceptance that she's really gone, or if it's some kind of revenge play that he'll wave in her face, should she ever return.

"Ooooo," she seethes aloud. "That ... that ...."

Wayne sets several of the crates near the dirt drive, then stalks to the barn.

"Boy, you did stick him good, didn't you?" Agnes points to the large bandages that are visible on both of Wayne's hands.

Sounds of a wagon being rolled into place drift through the barn door, followed by the sound of a horse being backed into place and then the clink of the hitching. After he pulls the wagon out to the yard, it takes Wayne about eight trips into the house to haul out the rest of the preserves. Since Amanda stole away on Duncan, he's forced to use their old plow horse to pull the wagon. As she watches the boxes, Amanda isn't sure whether to laugh or cry. It was hard work for her, doing all the slicing, boiling, and canning. Now he's going to enjoy the benefit of her labor. But she realizes she has no use for the sweet fruit anymore.

"The devil with it," she mutters. "Let him take the fruit and be gone."

"That's the spirit, dear."

He finishes loading the crates, throws in a few of her handmade quilts for good measure, and then climbs aboard.

It's just after sunrise when the iron-rimmed wooden wheels rattle down the driveway. Amanda waits until the dust has settled, then waits five minutes more. Then she runs out of the woods and down the hill toward the farm.

Thankfully the silverware remains up in the loft, right where she left it. Amanda counts out the pieces she managed to save: five spoons, seven forks, and eight knives. She cleaned most of the tarnish off the day after she found them. They're of excellent quality and should fetch a decent price if she can find the right place to sell them. She descends the ladder quickly, leaving her usual fear of heights behind. She pets each animal in the barn, bidding hasty good-byes and warning them not to make Wayne angry. She spends a special, quiet moment with Jessie. Noticing that she's heavy with milk because Wayne didn't take time for her this morning, she takes five minutes to empty the cow's swollen udder, expert hands finding a good quick rhythm. She leaves the bucket of milk for the barn cats to enjoy.

In the house, she locates her tattered suitcase and silently raids her own closest, taking her Sunday best, a shawl, some shoes, and a fancy purse she's never had occasion to use. She also stuffs in her best petticoats and then a few housedresses before heading to the dining room, squelching her desire to first rip Wayne's clothes to shreds.

Ever since she entered the front door, a certain temptation has been very strong for her. There is house silver too. Technically it's partly hers. It's not as fancy as the things she found. Most of it is just plated, but it's mildly desirable and certainly sellable. There are even a couple big serving spoons. She runs to the dining room and opens the small silver chest.

She looks at the gleaming set that she's always kept well polished and protected. She stares for half a minute.

No. She is not a thief. There are other ways to be resourceful. And why give Wayne a reason to accuse her? She'll come back later, with a lawyer if necessary, and argue about what rightfully belongs to her. For now, she'll simply take the one large serving spoon in the chest, the one that belonged to her aunt, and a sharp butcher knife. The knife isn't silver but it's nice-looking and it came from the kitchen of her childhood home. She also takes two small cut-glass decanters that were owned by her grandmother. Just her own things. That's all she wants. She also raids the tin can where she had set aside some money from the sale of her preserves. Stuffing that little bit of money in her pocket is actually the thing that makes her feel the most guilty. But Wayne was taking money from her too by stealing her preserves, wasn't he? She considers herself an honest woman. She's simply trying to make an honest departure.

Stepping through the door, suitcase in hand, she surveys the house and barn for one last time. There are things here that she will miss greatly, especially the animals and the wonderful peace she found while working in the kitchen and her backyard vegetable garden. She'll miss Wayne too, strangely. At least she'll miss what he used to be. And, dare she say it? She'll even miss the lovemaking. The way they stayed warm together in the winters. The slick sheen of sweat that formed between them in the summers. How does a proper lady ever put such a thought into words? And how does she ever find that again?

This part of her life, the time on the farm, is over. She blinks back tears.

"It isn't the leaving that bothers me so much," she tells the house and the grass. "It's the loss." She asks the yard a question that it can never answer. "What is it about me that I can't find my proper place on this earth? It wasn't in Boston, and I guess it's not here either."

What's next? Apparently it's returning to the place where she's already failed. And now, no friends and no family are there anymore. Why can't she find the right way to settle down? She can run away from Wayne, but she can't run away from herself.

Then she recalls when she stood, just a few days ago, on the sand near the ocean. There was an endless sea in front of her and a great vast country behind her. She's seen so little of this world. America, her own mysterious country, had grown so huge since she was a little girl. Somewhere in that enormity there must be a place for a women like her.

Somewhere. But she has no idea how to find that place.

Amanda turns to lock the door. What a strange thing to do since they haven't locked it in years. She holds a long iron key dangling from it. The only place she can think to hang the key is right from the locked doorknob. A message to Wayne that she's come and gone. Welcome back to your empty home.

She steps back to stare at the finality of the moment, suitcase on one side of her, pillowcase full of possessions on the other. So this is why some women stay with men they don't love. The emptiness of leaving can be even more crushing than just staying put.

Amanda catches a reflection in the glass. Up the hill, near the woods, Agnes waves frantically. She points down the road. Amanda turns to look and sees the familiar dust cloud rising. It can mean only one thing at this hour—Wayne is returning for something he forgot. He remains an unpredictable enigma right to the last.

Panic sets in. She looks toward Agnes, nodding. But she won't let the panic consume her. She won't yet run because there is one more thing she must do.

Running to the horse trough, she rolls up a sleeve and plunges her hand into the water. Feeling around, she shoves the large stone aside and watches the wooden puzzle box bob to the surface. Grabbing it, she tucks it into the top of the pillow case and runs up the hill toward Agnes. She's now a person who can carry all her earthly possessions in just two hands. It's a strange—and oddly liberating—feeling.

The baggage slows her. It bangs against thighs and drags on the grass.

"He's seen you!" Agnes shouts as Amanda staggers up the slope. The old woman runs down, grabbing the suitcase to lighten Amanda's load. Just as they reach the edge of the woods, the pillowcase rips.

Agnes wheezes as they drop to their knees. Gathering up the items, they spill them into an apron that Amanda ties off in a rough bundle.

"We must leave! Now!" Agnes shouts. "I could tell, just by the way he looked at you, that he's mad with rage!"

Amanda dives into the back bed of the carriage as Agnes staggers to the front driver's seat. With a cough the old women snaps the reins and wheels the cart through the trees, bouncing over rocks and roots. Amanda slides around in the bed of the wagon until they come out on the trail.

"Why did you have to grab that last thing out by the trough?" Agnes demands. "He might never have spotted you."

"It's important to me," she sputters, sitting up. "It just is." She looks around for one of the extra grain sacks they brought with them.

"So what is it?" Agnes shouts. "Is it that box you found? That one you saw at the beach?"

"Yes." She tries to crawl around the wagon to collect the bundle of items and the last few loose ones. The bumping and weaving sends her sprawling again.

Agnes shakes her head and shouts over her shoulder. "If he heads back up the road instead of heading to your house, he'll meet right up with us—probably right where this trail comes out. Is there any other way out of here?"

"No. This is the only path." Amanda braces her legs against the sides of the wagon as they round a slow curve. She removes the puzzle box from the bundle and places it in the sack, padding it the best she can with clothes. When she's done, she drags it with her as she pulls herself across the flatbed and up onto the buckboard, settling in beside Agnes. The old woman's white hair flows harpy-like behind her in the wind.

"If we can't avoid him, I guess we'll have to outrun him. Hang on!" She flicks the reins and sends the horses even faster down the path.

"Do you think we can?" Amanda shouts.

"Maybe we can. These are both good horses, and we know he has some weight in his wagon."

Amanda holds on, laughing out loud in spite of the danger. She laughs mostly at the spunk of this old woman and the folly of their situation. For some strange reason, she's starting to enjoy the ride.

They roar out of the woods and across a short field, merging onto the road. Wayne is indeed coming this way. His wagon is about 120 yards behind.

With a snap, he also makes his horse break from a fast trot to a full gallop. The poor horse strains at the weight of the cart it's pulling. Amanda looks back and sees the fury in his eyes. They have two horses and should be able to stay ahead of him. But so what? He'll remain close enough to follow their dust cloud and their tracks. He'll chase them all the way back to the Quincys' farm. Then he'll know where she's hiding. He'll know too much. And ...

*Did he pack his gun?*

They'll have to shake him somehow. Amanda looks around the cart for something to push into his path. She finds nothing. Sliding back into the bed of the wagon, she tries to pry up one of the floorboards. She could toss planks of wood at him. That might do something. But the boards won't budge. Then she has a far-fetched idea. A desperate idea really. Squatting there, in the bottom of the wagon, she finds a seam and tears away the bottom of her dress. She also tears away the bottom of her long petticoat. She throws them to the wind. They float near Wayne, but they fail to cover his face or the horse's face.

But that wasn't the main point of the idea. She then rolls up her sleeves and climbs back up to the front seat.

"What are you doing?" Agnes shouts over the bumps. She looks at Amanda like she's sitting next to a mad woman.

"We need to lose the wagon!" Amanda shouts. "We have to lighten the load, and we need to stop leaving wagon tracks. There are lots of horse prints in the road. We can blend into those. Wayne isn't a good enough tracker to be able to pick out our prints!" She smiles at Agnes. "Ever ride a horse bareback?"

Agnes shrieks. "You're crazy! I haven't ridden a horse at all since I was a girl."

"But are you with me? I'm not going to dump the wagon unless you agree. It's yours after all!"

Agnes stares straight ahead for a moment. Then a smile creeps over her face. She nods her approval and watches in fearful fascination as Amanda slides forward tentatively.

Holding her feedbag and suitcase, the young woman, now in a much shorter skirt, steps tentatively out onto the tongue of the wagon. Flopping the sack over the back of one of the horses, she tries to steady herself.

"You'll fall! You'll be killed!"

"He'll kill us too if he catches up! Come on! Step up! You can do it! I know you can."

Amanda tugs the reins from Agnes' hands. The horses feel nothing and continue on their fast, straight course down the road. The young woman uses the excess reins to hang her suitcase from one side of the horse. She uses a buckle to rip a small hole in the burlap then hangs the bag on the other side. Very makeshift saddle bags, but they'll do.

"You can do it!" she shouts back over her shoulder to Agnes.

"I can't!"

"Please! You can, and you must! If we leave the wagon, we're free!"

"I can't, dear! I'm an old woman."

"You can do more than you think. I already know that about you." She looks back, but sees Agnes shaking. With no reins to hold, her hands have found the sides of her head, and she holds onto herself in panic.

"Think of Elmer! He needs you!"

That comment stirs her a bit.

"And think of your life after Elmer!" Amanda shouts. "You're going to have to be tough from now on. Let's both start being tough right now!"

Amanda wonders for a moment if she's said the wrong thing. Perhaps the thought of life without her husband is enough to make Agnes give up, rather than press on. But the old woman suddenly leans forward, grasping the front board of the wagon. She slips out of her skirt. Then, freeing her legs by ripping off the bottom of her petticoat, she steps tentatively out onto the wooden wagon tongue between the two horses. Her face makes her look like a woman stepping onto thin ice atop a very deep pond.

Agnes throws her skirt into the air too, forcing Wayne to dodge it as it floats back. Amanda extends a hand, and soon Agnes has sidestepped all the way down the wagon tongue. With a boost from Amanda, she climbs aboard the horse on the right.

Ahead of them, the path narrows, heading down a small hill to the base of a narrow bridge. Amanda grins as she suddenly has an idea. This might be better than just abandoning the wagon, but she has to time it just right.

Behind them, Wayne whips his horse relentlessly and speeds toward them, gaining slightly. The crates of preserves bounce freely, and many of the jars break, glass bouncing out behind him like an ice storm.

Below Amanda is an iron pin that attaches the tongue to the rest of the wagon. Beneath the tongue is a clip that holds the pin in place. She squats, carefully … carefully, feeling along the bottom. She finds the clip and has to yank it hard before it pulls free. She then unhooks two leather straps.

The next part will be tricky. She swallows hard, stands atop the iron pin, and grabs onto the collar of the horse on the left. Pinching the big pin between her feet, she tries to lift herself up and onto the horse. The pin doesn't pull free at first. There's too much weight pinching it in place. But a few bumps and bounces help wiggle the connection, and she, in turn, wiggles the pin upwards. It suddenly pulls free. As Amanda drags herself upwards, the wagon starts to pull free.

But there's a snag in her plans. The wooden tongue has two parts, half attached to the horses and half attached to the wagon. A strap hitches the two together. It's a safety feature in case the pin ever comes loose—just like now.

Agnes reaches into her bodice and produces a tiny folding knife. She hands it to Amanda.

"Never mind why," she says to Amanda's astonished look. "Just use it!"

Amanda slides off the horse, back down to the wood. She doesn't dare place much weight on it, so she steadies herself by again hanging onto the bouncing horse collar. The animals thunder on, barely aware of her presence.

As she stretches down to cut the strap, the wood pieces start to sag. If the tongue drops too soon, it will dig in, halting their progress and probably hurting the horses. It can't drop to the ground until the strap is cut clean through. Amanda lifts with all her might, supporting the wood with her ankle as she hangs from the horse like a trapeze artist. She cuts away the strap just as they approach the bridge. Transferring her weight to the horse collar, she kicks what's left of the rigging backwards, almost falling in the process. The heavy wagon tongue crashes down just behind the rear hooves of the heavy horses. Swaying wildly Amanda claws her way back up onto the horse, pinching the animal's neck hard with her legs to keep from bouncing off.

They picked up considerable momentum coming down the hill. Amanda had hoped to make it roll to a stop near the bridge, but as the tongue drops to the road it digs in hard. The wagon slows quickly. Then something unexpected happens. Then wagon tongue buries itself deep into the dirt just as the horse, the women, and what's left of the front part of the rigging accelerate and pull clear.

The whole wagon flips high and careens end over end. The sound makes Amanda feel like she's running away from a collapsing building. After two and a half bounces the wagon shatters on the roadway, leaving a shower of iron and boards on the road and spilling onto the bridge. A single surviving wheel rolls on, eventually veering off into the creek.

As the women, petticoats flying, ride quickly away up the road, they laugh openly. They did it. And now, as long as they can hang onto the oversized horse yokes, they're safe.

Because the horses are still hitched together, they ride in tandem, but even in this awkward state they still should be able to outrun him.

Wayne pulls his own wagon to a stop behind the shattered rig. The main bed of the wagon, what's left of it, blocks his access to the bridge. Even if he wanted to drag it out of the way, he knows he'll never catch them now. He doesn't even have time to unhook his horse and climb aboard, mimicking his wife's escape. Through squinted eyes, he views the pair galloping away, horses hooked together with a lattice of straps and chains between them. He curses, spits on the ground, and bids Amanda good riddance.

# Chapter 18

## *Business*

Devlin Richards likes to sit close to a candle when he talks business. He draws it slowly toward him from the center of the table, letting it sit about three inches from his folded hands. Today the knuckles on those hands are puffier than they should be, bloodied and bruised just enough for a sharp eye to notice.

The candlelight shines directly up at him casting harsh shadows that oddly distort his face, making him look ominous and maybe even dangerous. The candle is a handy tool that he discovered many years ago, but few people seem to take such advantage of its power.

If negotiations go well, Devlin may slowly push the candle back toward the center, taking on a more friendly tone and a less treacherous look. Sometimes he even blows out the candle and orders drinks. The mood changes.

But if negotiations do not go well, if prices seem too high or if promises seem broken, he slowly leans over the candle as he talks. That's the time to lay on the southern accent heavy and thick, just to seem all the more eccentric and dangerous to these Yankees. Shadows grow harsher. Uneasiness lingers. He lets the smoke that rises from the cheap tallow curl up and around his face, until his fearsome image burns into the subconscious of the person on the other end of the negotiations. With the help of a simple candle, Devlin issues his warning and slowly extracts the type of deal he desires.

Tonight at The Rose Point he has the candle very close. The smoke, which would sting the eyes of most men, seems to have little effect on Devlin. It dances and cups around his face, blackening the edges of his cheeks.

"What is it that you don't understand?" he asks, soul afire. "I said I'm not the man you need for your little job, my good man, and you don't offer enough anyway. Now, I've asked you once to leave my table, haven't I? I'm starting to wonder, in spite of your clean clothes and refined manner …," he leans low over the flickering light, "just how wise a man you really are."

Across the filthy table, located near the smoky rear of The Rose Point, sits a man named Jeb Thomas. Devlin has seen him before. In fact he is the man in work clothes—surprisingly clean work clothes—who had stood near the same table two nights before, keenly listening to the same stories as Devlin. Now here he is again. And the trick of the candle doesn't seem to faze him.

Jeb smiles at Devlin, rolls a cigarette, and picks up the candle to light it. He then sets the candle well aside, replacing Devlin's sinister smoky haze with one of his own. He exhales a bitter cloud of tobacco.

"I guess I'm wise enough to know that we will make a deal, and that I don't need to slink away, much as you might want that."

"You are a very foolish man," Devlin says with a raised but carefully controlled voice. "I wonder how long that will last?"

Jeb Thomas shrugs. "Perhaps, Mr. Richards," he says through smoky breath, "you should instead wonder about what happened to Mr. Rudolph Baines, a man who was murdered after leaving here the other night. I certainly know what happened to him. I have a keen sense that you might know too."

Devlin sits back slightly, but his look doesn't change.

"You know, Mr. Richards, I really wanted to talk with that man. So I followed him, just as you did. But while you had robbery on your mind, I had other plans." Jeb shakes his head. "Unfortunately, you spoiled those plans when you put a knife into Mr. Baines. How unfortunate."

They stare directly into each other's eyes. Then they look around, to see who else is within earshot. Fortunately the noise of the pub absorbs any words that drift beyond the tabletop.

"I don't know what you are talking about," Devlin sneers.

"Yes, you do."

Devlin leans forward, grabs the candle, and snuffs it out with his fingers. "You, sir, are on dangerous ground. If you think you know something, then you also must know that such things are usually best kept to one's self. Perhaps you have made a serious mistake."

Jeb leans forward too, nearly daring Devlin to blink. He whispers, low enough so the noise of the crowd nearly swallows the whole of his voice, "This is OUR secret. I know what you have done. I'm sure you already have realized that I have my reasons for not turning you in. I would have done so by now, don't you think? In fact, Mr. Richards, I have reason to hire a man of your skill. I should think that alone might be the basis for an interesting partnership."

Devlin looks back. "So far I've heard no offer that attracts my interest. I don't care what you think or what you know. I don't tend to enter into business partnerships with damn Yankees." He squints, then hisses, "You can be dealt with."

"I did mention money earlier. Let's consider that only the start. I'm looking for a sailor. One in particular. If we could find him and … um … extract the proper information, your reward could be substantially higher."

Devlin's voice slides out through clenched teeth. "And you are foolish enough to think I'd work on speculation for a man I don't know? Especially one who is trying to blackmail me? I should think, if you now know my reputation, that you'd see the problem y'all have just created for yourself."

Jeb Thomas pauses to consider this. "Well, more than anything, I think you are a businessman. And also a risk taker. Let me explain why I want to find this sailor, and then you decide. If it's not for you, just walk away. I swear I won't contact the authorities about what I saw."

Devlin gives a cold look, but listens.

"We both stood here listening to stories about the ship that went down. Did you know the *Gossamer* visited South Africa just before its final voyage?"

No response. Jeb decides to take his time, so he cleans the edge of a fingernail before continuing. "Well, she did. She stopped in Port Elizabeth, month before last. Took on raw sugar cane, big bales of wool too. And something else."

He finally catches Devlin's eye again. Jeb reaches over, shoving the annoying candle to the side. "Do you know what it's like over there, Mr. Richards? There's diamonds. There in the ground, diamonds big as your damn balls. They come out raw, but after that? Cut, uncut, polished or not. Rocks are the second currency over there. And those diamonds come cheap to men who know how and what to trade."

Devlin nods slowly.

"Locals come down to the ships to make their trades. I was there a few years ago. You ought to see it someday if you can. Black faces in the night. Mouths and noses covered with greasy bandanas. They come looking to swap diamonds and gold for guns. They come late at night, right up to the piers. In the north, part of the country the Xhosa are always fighting the Zulu. Hell, some group is always fighting another. No fucking clue why. But when it comes to battle, they mean business."

"Where do they get the diamonds?"

"I don't know. I guess some of them work in the mines. When you're down there deep, a few of the rocks can find their way into pockets or shoes when no one is looking. Other rocks may be bought on the cheap or stolen. I don't know. All I do know is that a man with a forty-dollar gun in his locker can trade that gun for a $400 diamond just like that. And no one is the wiser. He can trade other things too for smaller diamonds—clothes, hats, tools. I know of a man unbolted a ship's compass and traded it not for a diamond but for a chunk of gold. Turned out to be worth over $4,000. Not worth that much to them, but certainly worth that much back here."

Devlin nods slightly. "I've heard such stories too. What's your point?"

"The point, my dear future associate, is that I have a friend whose ship was in port the same day as the *Gossamer* before the *Gossamer* headed out on its final trip. He saw a couple of the sailors near the pier who were doing business with a group of local men. What they were offering was substantial. No big gems, but hundreds of small ones. Bags of them. Who knows what they might be worth here, but I'm guessing tens of thousands of dollars. Maybe more."

Devlin retains his skeptical face, but his interest level has obviously risen a bit. Jeb can see that.

"So what? Even if I did believe you, the rocks would be long gone by now. The ship sailed into Boston and then it left again. I'm quite sure whatever they had on board was sold when they were in port."

"You would think so, wouldn't you? But I don't believe that's the case, and here's why." Jeb slowly sits back. He'd been a fisherman once, years ago. Thus he knows how to place his hook expertly. Now it's just a matter of reeling Devlin in, slowly and carefully. The challenge is, this particular fish is a shark, and Jeb needs to be extra careful and crafty.

Jeb waits just long enough, so he can see Devlin fidget slightly fighting the urge to ask. Jeb can tell that just asking would show a level of interest that Devlin would much rather mask.

"Do you know what business I'm in, Mr. Richards?" Jeb continues.

"You're a labor organizer. I know that much," Devlin sneers. "You try to unionize workers at the docks. You wear the uniform of a typical dock worker. Not sure if you've ever done a lick of work yourself though. Have you?"

"I have. And you're correct about what I do. I know a lot about what the laborers at the docks are up to. And most of them come to realize, sooner or later, that I'm a man who looks out for them. That's how I knew about the *Gossamer* in the first place. You see, the ship of another friend of mine left South Africa a couple days ahead of them. I knew what dock they were going to pull up to long before she ever broke over the horizon. I was waiting for what she was carrying. I was waiting for those diamonds, Mr. Richards. But unlike the gems that were being shopped around the waterfront, the diamonds I was looking for never made it to shore."

"What makes you so sure?"

"Because there were police on the docks waiting for them. And men from the customs house. It was too hot to bring them out. Also, a man who was carrying them was in some sort of trouble on board. He wasn't allowed to get off the ship, so the diamonds stayed on board."

"Oh, come on. There's a thousand ways to sneak them off."

"I know the man who was waiting for them. I know the conversations that he had. His contact, the man who carried them, worked in the engine room. He had extra duties and no shore time while in port. So he didn't meet his connection. Just made some hand signals to the buyer from the deck. The *Gossamer*'s next run was just going over and back. Twenty-some days, tops. Using hand signals, they simply agreed to meet again. That buyer pays the best prices. He knew the sailor would wait for the deal, so they agreed to wait and …."

"And then they sank to the bottom of the Atlantic," Devlin finished the sentence. "End of story. End of the diamonds, assuming your story is even true."

"So you would think. But my friend told me where those diamonds were. He told me about waterproof boxes that some of the sailors had, stashed beneath their berths. Boxes that are meant to float." Jeb's voice drops to a conspiratorial whisper. "Can I confide in you? I have to tell you, Mr. Richards, there isn't a lot of money for a man like me who works as a labor organizer. Business owners chase you away. Workers don't always trust you. You have to live on the donations that laborers are willing to pay. I've been beat up more times than I can count. So why do I continue? I try to organize dockworkers because I think it's the right thing to do. I feel good about it. But I have to be honest. It's only my side deals that keep me going. Little deals along the way are what keep food on my table. I justify the shady exchanges by the good that I do in return. A lot of labor work to do good for a lot of men. And their families. Make sense?"

He studies Devlin and realizes that the words are lost to him. Devlin is not a man who worries about moral justification. Any deal is the right deal.

"Well, anyway, the reason I believe this story is real is that I have some experience at listening to such talk. Eventually a man like me learns who to ignore and who to listen to when visiting a port city. All I can say is that I believed this man. He waited near the ship with me. He had his reasons for sharing the information. I was going to be a sales channel. I travel all over the country. I have to deal with rich and poor.

"Another thing, he was particularly interested in talking to a different man too. That man was getting *on*, not off the ship. That man mostly stayed on the deck while they were in port, fiddling with some equipment he brought with him. Strangest thing I've seen."

Devlin nods. "That sailor who was running his yap in here a few nights ago. He mentioned that man too. Said he was a scientist."

"Yes. I think it's the same one."

"So let's say all of this is true," Devlin grunts, "which I doubt. The ship is still on the bottom of the sea now. What good is any of this?"

"The ship broke apart. Much of it washed ashore. I can't help but wonder if some of those waterproof boxes could have survived."

Devlin shrugs. "Sounds far-fetched."

"Perhaps. But I have my reasons for thinking so. I don't play odds blindly, and I don't think you do either."

Devlin sits silently for several moments, staring at the tabletop. "Okay. I will admit that I'm intrigued. But what is it you want me to do?"

"I need muscle. We need to ask some questions."

"I'm not intrigued enough to work on speculation. You know my rates. I'll ask around, find out what I can, and we'll talk. I expect at least sixty dollars for my trouble, and $125 if I deliver useful information to you."

"I think that sounds fair."

"And when you find the diamonds, I want half of them."

"Twenty percent."

Devlin's eyes narrow. "And you are a little fuck. You don't think I can just take them all if I want? You're lucky I'm not cutting you out of this venture right now!"

"Twenty-five percent. Best I can do. I have to use some of those diamonds for bribes. Business, you understand."

"Thirty-five. No less."

And just like that, they reach their agreement and shake hands.

"The first thing we should do," says Devlin, "is to find that sailor again. I haven't seen him in the pubs since then. But he must be around somewhere. I don't think he was in any shape to ship out again."

Jeb orders two whiskeys and pulls a dollar coin from his shirt pocket. Devlin still thinks that shirt looks far too clean.

"As you can see, I don't travel with as much money as our dear departed Mr. Baines. But this dollar should buy us another couple rounds."

Devlin smirks. The barkeep relights their candle, and they drink and plot until that candle burns low.

# Chapter 19

## *Steam*

Elmer Quincy surprises himself as he moves around inside his faded gray barn. He kicks the chocks out from beneath the wheels of his aging steam wagon and even finds enough strength in his thin body to give it a mighty shove. The cast-iron water tank is only about one-eighth full. The sloshing motion in the nearly empty cylinder actually helps him get the wagon moving, thanks to a few good rocks. With a final slosh, the contraption rolls out the barn door and down a short earthen ramp. It slows to a stop about twelve yards away, leaving behind a trail of coal dust and rust flakes.

Whistling happily, Elmer loads the vehicle's burner with several shovels full of coal—the cheap, smoky kind with brownish flecks and glass-green veins sprinkled throughout.

In a bin behind the front seat, he slowly loads another sixty pounds of coal until his arms ache and he can't lift another shovel.

Moving slowly now, he pours a cup of kerosene into the burner, then strikes a white-headed wooden match on the rough tank. Tossing it in, he watches the fire catch. With a few wheezing breaths he bends low and forces the fresh fire down deep into the coals. In five minutes, he hears the *tink* of the water tank starting to expand. This is followed by the low simmer of water heating. Satisfied, Elmer seals the valve on the top of the tank then sits down, exhausted.

Settling back into the driver's seat, he watches the pressure gauge slowly climb. The calm of the morning is interrupted as his wife and Amanda come thundering into the barnyard. Barely dressed, they're laughing, sitting atop the horses that are not pulling the wagon they left with. The women tug at the horses, trying to get them to stop. It takes one long loop around the yard before both of the horses halt.

"What the hell are you doing?" Elmer yells. "Where's the wagon?"

The horses stumble toward the water trough, where they drink heartily. The women slide down, Amanda helping Agnes as she wavers and shakes. Then they laugh again, realizing what a sight they must be without their dresses.

Agnes looks to Elmer and notices he's staring openly at Amanda, who's showing more skin then he's ever seen on a woman other than his wife.

"Elmer? Elmer! Dear, what are you doing with the steam wagon?"

He swallows hard and looks back to his wife. Agnes shoos Amanda toward the house to find some decent clothes.

"What? Oh ... I ... I don't think we can spare a horse right now."

"I've already told her she can take one of the horses, Elmer. You know that. She offered to trade her horse for it. He'll be healed soon."

"Yes, I know. But I want her to take this instead. We have a big farm and only two horses for our nephews to use. We really could use another horse, and I have no use for this crazy thing anymore." He looks toward the steam wagon with a forlorn look. "I mean ... you won't have any use for it. Not me."

She looks at Elmer and shakes her head. "Are you daft? That thing is a death trap." She points to the set of levers near the dashboard. "Besides, she doesn't know how to run it. Look at all the controls. Get one wrong, and there's too much pressure. No, that thing is too dangerous."

"Nonsense," Elmer scoffs. "I learned how it works, didn't I? She can learn too. She's a smart woman."

"Why don't we just put her on the train?"

Before responding, he asks her several questions about what happened to the wagon, and he learns about the chase and their escape.

"Well, then, doesn't that rule out the train?"

"Why?"

"Because her husband will be looking for her there! Maybe the police too. Where else would she go if she's going to run? He'll tell the ticket agent to send a boy to fetch the town constable if she shows up. They'll all think she stole something from the home. Think about it. You know that will be his story after today. She's from away, so people will believe him too, especially when they see the cuts she said she left on his hands. If they find her carrying anything, she'll be arrested sure as the world."

"It's her own home, Elmer! You can't be arrested for breaking into your own home, can you?"

"I know that. And maybe they do too. But I bet they'll arrest her anyway and let the judge work it out. Add an assault charge, and she's not in good shape at all, in the court's eyes."

Agnes nods and looks toward the wagon, which seems to be coming to a full boil.

"I need to get more water in there," Elmer says.

"We really should just let her stay here," Agnes replies.

"Well, we've both told her that. But she won't stay. She wants to go back to the city, and it's probably a good idea for her to put some distance between her and that crazy husband. Things just didn't work out for her here, shame to say. At least one of our neighbors is already talking about the fact that we have a woman living here. Word will get out after today's chase. He'll find her here."

Agnes nods again. The wagon continues to steam. "Well, I think it's a crazy idea just to give this contraption to her. But I certainly won't miss it. Blasted thing has always scared the daylights out of me."

Amanda emerges from the house. Looking at the wagon, she grins, remembering their adventures during the trip to the beach. "Are you taking it out again, Elmer?"

Elmer and Agnes exchange glances.

"Actually, we'd like to give it to you," Elmer says.

Amanda blinks, hand traveling to her mouth as she smiles. "What? This? You can't! It's a treasure!"

"It's a menace," Agnes replies. "It really should just be driven into the ocean."

Elmer calls Amanda over. "I'd really rather give you this than a horse. My family has no use for it anymore. It's just a toy, while we always need good horses."

He watches her gaze travel along its length with a look of fear and fascination in her eyes. "I couldn't."

"It will get you out of town pretty fast, dear. Faster than anything else you could ride."

"I don't even know how to run it."

"I can teach you."

They argue. She resists, but Agnes and Elmer can see that she's fascinated by the idea. There are only a handful of automobiles in the state and can't be more than one or two women in Massachusetts who have ever driven one. Does this thing even qualify as an automobile? It's old and rusty and steamy and strange.

Finally she accepts, with the understanding that she will return it to them somehow, someday. With that, they load her bags and sacks into the back. The last thing to go in is the puzzle box. Amanda smiles as she sees Elmer look it over. "Interesting little thing, isn't it?" she says.

Elmer struggles to remember something, then smiles. "I was in Boston years ago, and I remember stopping into a curiosity shop that had several of these things for sale. They came in all shapes and styles and none of them were exactly like this one."

"Really? There are other boxes like this?"

"I'm not sure how similar they are. But the owner of the shop, a Chinaman, seemed to have a special interest in collecting them. He showed me how some of them opened."

Amanda quickly picks the box up and hands it to him. "Maybe you know a trick to open this one. I'm kind of stuck."

She shows him how to open the first two levels. Elmer studies the next level for nearly a minute, then points to a corner of the panel.

"See right there? See how this area just looks like part of the grain of the wood? But there's a tiny outline around that part. It's a trick. It's really a thin curved slot with the grain painted on. You'll need a fingernail, longer than mine. Just press right there ...."

He holds the box firmly while Amanda inserts a fingernail, a nail that's neatly trimmed but with no polish. She presses down and hears a tiny click. Elmer puts his thumb against the panel and slides it toward him. Narrow rubber seals squeak as they part. The compartment underneath is larger than the two she's opened so far. It's nearly a half inch deep. There's a small leather-bound book there. She plucks it out delicately, as if she's lifting a piece of glass.

Agnes and Elmer gather close as she opens the book and runs a finger over the name that's written there. *Victor Marius.* They flip through the first few pages and see dates and writing. It appears to be a journal.

"He must be the owner of the box," she says. "Those initials are on the front. He must have put this journal in here to keep it safe. She turns some more pages and begins reading one of the several entries. It mentions boredom and the passage of time on the seas. She flips to the front of the book and sees that he wrote down his thoughts through a previous voyage. That trip must have been taken a few months before. After he returned to Boston, the entries became shorter and less frequent. No surprise there. He must have had other things to do while ashore. Suddenly she snaps the book shut, feeling like she's been caught peeping into someone's window.

"It's okay, dear," Agnes assures her. "He's dead. This is a bit of history that you've found."

"But still ...."

"Think about it. He wouldn't have put it in there if he didn't want someone to find it!"

"Take it with you," Elmer says in a calm tone. "Read it when you're ready. You know where it sits in the box and how to get to it." With that, he places the small book back into the box, slides the rubber-sealed pieces back into place, and relocks all the compartments.

They climb aboard. Elmer sits in the driver's seat, playing instructor. Except that it's not really a seat at all. The steering lever is so tall that he has to nearly stand to use it. Both Elmer and Amanda lean back against what is basically a tall bench that looks like something a warehouse shipping clerk would use.

To set the car in motion, Elmer shows her the proper order for using the levers. He also turns a nozzle to redirect some of the steam. With a hiss the car jerks forward a bit, an angry tiger on a leash. "Oops."

He then presses a clutch and engages the main lever. As he releases the clutch, the wagon groans and slowly starts forward, gathering steam as Elmer pilots it out of the yard. With each turn of the wheel, water in the tank splashes against the hot sides, making a low hiss. As they pick up speed, the hisses start to blend together into one long murmur.

"There's two main pistons," he points and yells above the noise. "One on either side, just like a train. Each stroke of the pistons bleeds just a tiny bit of the pressure. The pistons crank the two big wheels on the sides. He points to one of the wheels, but it's spinning so fast it's all just a big blur to Amanda.

Out on the road, Elmer stops and starts the wagon several times, showing her how it's done, going over each of the levers, explaining how they work; showing her what to look for, how to know if there's too much pressure or too little. "Be good to her," he smiles. "And careful too. This buggy is old and cranky, just like Agnes."

Eventually Amanda takes the wheel. The wagon lurches and sputters as she tries to get the feel of the controls. At one point the tank blows off a huge cloud of steam, and Amanda apologizes, thinking she broke something.

"Don't worry about it, dear. It's just a safety valve. We have all the steam we need right now."

Eventually she gets the starting and stopping part down. She can make the transition smoothly. But the steering is tough. She has to pull hard to turn the wheels, and she oversteers terribly. It's a challenge just to stay on the road.

"Believe it or not, the faster you go the easier it is to steer. When you get out on the open road, don't be afraid to open her up."

They run for a bit then Elmer points to a small trail that leads down near the railroad tracks. "Head down there. There's a spring and a small water tower next to the tracks. The water tower has a swing arm. That's usually where I go to fill this car."

"Can we do that?"

"Bah. The railroad won't miss the water. I only take about a third of the tank and it will refill itself in a few hours."

Amanda bites her lip. It's a narrow path, little more than a couple of ruts for wagon wheels. She slows down, in spite of Elmer's warnings, and it takes nearly twenty minutes for her to oversteer all the way to the end. Then it takes another twenty minutes to fill their big water tank. Elmer takes the controls, but he's not able to line the steam wagon up just right. There's a fresh pile of coal next to the tower. Eventually they just pile up some dirt and branches so that they can drive onto the tracks instead. Then they have to blow off some of the pressure before they can open the big hatch and let the water in.

"This is the risky part," Elmer confides. "Once you lose the steam, you don't have any power, so you can't move. I hate having to drive onto the track like this. There's no way off until you build up your pressure again." His eyes scan up and down the track, and he listens intently over the sound of the flowing water.

Luckily, no trains come. They finish filling, close the valves, let the pressure slowly build again, and they're able to drive off after a few minutes. Amanda runs back to clear the branches away from the tracks.

They spend the rest of the afternoon on backroads and fields, with Elmer teaching and re-teaching Amanda to drive, shift, and steer. "See the steering mechanism?" he says, pointing to a shaft and attached handles poking up through the floor. "It's a double-thread screw shaft. And see here?

This connects to a swiveling ball joint near the sprung front axle."

His words are like some foreign language, but she forces herself to listen.

"If you move it just this way, it's a bit easier to steer. I learned that the hard way, let me tell you."

He smiles as they whisk down a long dirt road. "It's grand, I tell you. What an engineer the person was who designed this. What a man ahead of his time! Twenty-five years before we started seeing other kinds of automobiles. Can you believe that?"

He points down toward the bottom of the ball joint. "But see here too? It's worn. I think that's part of the reason why you're oversteering, dear. Because of that worn spot it doesn't react quickly. It doesn't catch until you've turned it too far. Then you have to correct. Just be aware of that."

Amanda nods, trying to take it all in.

By late afternoon, she's gained confidence as she stops, starts, and turns many times. She learns how to light the fire and put it out. She learns how to build up the steam and tweak the valves to keep things working at their peak. She gives a little squeal of delight each time the wagon lurches anew down the road. This is the best adventure she's had since her trip to the beach and the shipwreck.

Eventually they return to the water tower for more water, then back to the house for supper. Before they go inside, Elmer shows her about one more little glitch. It's the one she saw the Quincys experience that day on the beach. "Keep this in mind too. If the cart bumps too hard, things can get knocked out of alignment," he says. "So this valve needs to be shut off while this pipe here," he taps on it, "is pulled backwards. You see?" He shows her how to make the adjustment. "Temperamental damn thing!"

His wife joins them, and the three make plans for Amanda to leave in the middle of the night. At a steady thirty miles per hour, she can get to Boston, in theory, in a bit over four hours. It will probably take longer because the roads aren't always smooth. She'll also have to stop for water at least once, so they plan on a five-hour trip, just to be safe. Elmer worries about the excitement a steam car will create, so they agree she should arrive early in the morning, right around sunup if possible. She'll be able to see where she's going, but by the time people rise from bed to see what's causing all the noise, she'll already be a block away.

After supper Agnes rides a little one-horse surrey into town. She sends a telegraph to her cousin, Beverly Morgan, who lives in the city's North End. The Morgan family has a carriage house behind their home, and she asks if Amanda can hide the car there after her arrival. Maybe Beverly can also give Amanda a bed for a few nights?

The reply comes back in the early evening, carried out to the farm by a telegraph boy on horseback. Beverly says she welcomes a chance to help Amanda. Anything for dear old Agnes and Elmer.

So everything is set. Amanda is just a few hours from making her escape. She lies down, but her attempt at sleep is restless. So many unknowns. So unclear where things are heading. She's about to drive off into the dark, toward a vague destination, sitting atop a boiling and sparking beast that she's not even sure she can trust.

# Chapter 20

## *Scrutiny*

A pair of dice thrown onto the deck of a ship during rough seas may be the most honest roll made in any dice game. The sway of the floor makes it hard to cheat. Dice bounce differently. Unpredictably. On land, some gamblers master their own special drop or a creative backhanded throw. It gives them an edge. But such talents are useless when playing on a ship. The unpredictable nature of such games make them seem more honest and more tempting to those who watch. And men grow bored with the monotony of a long voyage. A dice game promises excitement, camaraderie, and a thin promise of riches. The game is the flame, and the sailors are the moths.

The men who have lost at shipboard gambling are easy to spot. Nursing their anger, they'll huddle with other losers back on shore to pool their limited funds. They buy a couple bottles of cheap wine and gather on the docks rather than at the dockside pubs. Their shore leave is more subdued than what the winners enjoy. Coils of ropes and tin buckets become their seats. Empty wooden crates become tables. A bottle passes, and so does the time.

Yet, after days or weeks at sea, there is some level of pleasure in just being ashore. A dock doesn't rock like a ship's deck. So they drink. They talk. They laugh. Then they argue about what might have been if the dice rolled the other way. They think about how close they came, and they talk about what life might be like if luck smiles on them the next time.

Devlin Richards seldom plays dice or cards, but he knows how to mingle with gamblers. He likes the way they spend money if they win. He likes the way they shoot their mouths off if they lose. And if they're foolish enough to walk alone, he knows what to take and how to take it from them.

It doesn't matter if the docks are located in New England or South Carolina; Devlin has learned how to visit the small groups of losers who gather on the docks. He throws in a few coins and shares in the bottle. He listens to the stories and slowly gains their confidences. He hears things. Some of the information is useful immediately, and some is filed away for later. On the morning of June 25, he stands with a small group of unshaven sailors near Boston's Rowes Wharf. Early drinkers all, they talk of hauling heavy cargo, fishing, and the problem they see with the damn immigrants who will work for practically nothing. Devlin slowly prods the conversation in a new direction. The wreck. It's becoming old news, but it still draws comments. What have they heard? What about the sailor who survived? Anyone seen him lately? Any details about the things that floated ashore?

Yeah, they've all heard the scuttlebutt. No, not sure how much of it is true.

Devlin pulls a small bottle of coveted single-malt Scotch whiskey out of his coat pocket and starts passing it around. This is the stuff the rich boys drink. They all want a taste.

Soon more details spill out.

"I don't know," shrugs the one with the gray beard. "Now I heard this all secondhand. Ya have to understand that."

"Of course," Devlin nods. "It's just interesting, you know? To be plucked from death like that. If he's one of the survivors, he's a lucky man, wouldn't y'all say?"

"Yes, I would. I would indeed," graybeard says, scratching his whiskers. "So that man you say you met in the pub? Another one from the *Gossamer*?"

"Yes."

"I'd say God grabbed his ass before the devil could grab his ankles to pull him under. That's what I'd say." The whole group laughs.

Devlin laughs too and takes a swig from the bottle as it passes by.

"The way I hear tell though," the old man says, "he was a deckhand, not one of the black gang. He was topside, and apparently he grabbed a hammer and some nails before the ship went down. When one of crates floated free, he grabbed it and nailed the sleeve of his coat right onto the wood. Guess he figured it would keep him attached to the thing even if he passed out."

Devlin looks confused but says nothing.

"I'll have to remember that trick," one of the sailors said.

"Oh horseshit," said another. "What if the crate takes on water and starts to sink? What are you going to do then? Sounds like a risky move to me."

"Yes, and what if you die while floating?" Devlin adds. "Imagine finding a floating dead man, nailed to a box like that. Wouldn't that be a wretched thing to find?"

"I'd be cursed, ever I find something like that on the water," says one of the men.

Graybeard nods. "Can't say as I disagree. But I guess it worked for him. Story is that he floated for two days. He must have slept some of that time, I'd think. But he was mostly awake when a freighter found him. Couldn't pull him free though, so they had to haul him and the crate up together with a winch."

Devlin elects to speak up. "That's a much different story than the one told by the guy I met."

The old man gives Devlin a hurt look. "What's that then? You don't believe us?"

"Just that I met that sailor at a pub near here, and he told it a lot different. Said he hung on to some boards, not that he nailed his clothes to a crate. Described his rescue different too. And he said it was him and the cook together."

"Maybe I'm not talking about him."

Devlin raises an eyebrow.

"How about that," a younger sailor snorts. "You think a third sailor survived too?"

More sipping, laughing, and cursing by the other men.

"Yeah, well, I wouldn't know about who lived and who didn't. It's just something I heard. Take it or leave it."

Devlin squints at the man. "So who told you all this?"

"Mate a' mine who was on the freighter that picked him up. When they came back from the deep water, they pulled around Oak Bluff and into Steamboat Wharf."

"Nantucket?"

"A-yeah."

"So definitely *was* a different sailor. Did they take him ashore there?"

"They did."

"The crate too?"

The whole group laughs at this.

"How the hell should I know?"

Devlin feels a spike of anger but controls it. He decides to change the subject, asking about the weather, and making small talk about the other tiny islands that are closer to the Boston Harbor. Eventually he approaches the subject of the *Gossamer* again.

"I'll tell ya," he says, "if I'm ever plucked from the ocean like that, I hope to end up somewhere less godforsaken than Nantucket. Two days? No food or water? Bashed around like that? I'd hope for a good hospital instead."

"Oh, they took him to a doctor at least. The doc wasn't on the island the day they pulled in. So a day later, they loaded him on a skiff headed into Falmouth. So he's on the mainland now, at a boarding house there. Still under a doctor's care, way I hear it. Must have been in damn bad shape."

"How do you know all this?"

"Well, funny thing. My friend on the freighter had some pretty vivid details. Said just seeing that made him want to quit sailing. A quick up and back to Nova Scotia for a load of coal, he says, then he's going to end it. Guy was sort of pale and broken up. Looked like a man run over by a train. Like a ghost. A man don't forget something like that."

"No. I guess he doesn't."

Devlin presses for more details, but he sees distrust in their eyes when he seems to be pressing too hard. He's gleaned all the information he can from this group. When the bottle is finished, he moves on. The information is useful though. A third survivor? Maybe a surviving crate? It's good news, and Jeb Thomas damn well better pay him a few dollars to hear the particulars.

Before heading to The Rose Point, he walks over to the lab of the dead sailor. It's his second trip to the place since he was able to glean its location from the young boys on the dock. On his previous visit, he'd managed to slip inside and steal a cutting torch and some tools, which he sold for seven dollars. No one seemed to notice his visit. Apparently no one is keeping an eye on the place.

But maybe he assumed too much. This time he finds the windows boarded up and the front door padlocked shut. So his previous intrusion must have been detected by the landlord after all.

Devlin finds something to pry off a few boards—just enough to slip inside. Feeling around in the dark, he fashions a makeshift torch out of a stick and a rag then lights it so that he can see the room.

There's still a great deal of equipment here. Unusual, expensive-looking stuff. But he doesn't have any idea how to find a buyer for these specialty items.

Devlin sorts through the equipment for nearly an hour, exasperated that he has to keep making new torches to see what he's doing. His work produces little in the way of results. There's a small electric motor he may be able to sell, some additional hand tools, and a crate of light bulbs.

There are so many chemicals and mysterious small parts. He knows they must have value, but it's frustrating not to have any sort of market to unload them.

When he's gathered all he can, he sets his items outside. In a final act of frustration and anger, he knocks over three containers of liquid and sets his torch to them. He's not even sure if they're flammable. They are. In fact, they take flame so quickly that he barely has time to squeeze back out the window before the whole room is engulfed.

Carrying his slim pickings in a small box, Devlin steals quickly away. The street is well lit by the rising flames behind him. He holds less than twenty dollars' worth of items while the remains of the dead scientist's lab burn brightly in the night.

# Chapter 21

## *Sparks*

Dark sometimes is described as the absence of light. But light, conversely, is not just the absence of dark. Light is something far different.

With light comes particles and power, and things still unknown to man. Light has mysterious, wonderful properties. It can be created, amplified, reflected, fractured, and bent in ways that darkness can never comprehend.

Light is energy. Darkness is but a void.

In the earliest days of commercial electricity, the modest goal was simply to create artificial light. Bring in light to chase away the void of darkness so that the day can continue. And work can too, sometimes far into the night.

A certain box-like building on the outskirts of Pittsburgh, Pennsylvania, often remains illuminated until midnight or later. Deep inside this place there are men, driven as much by curiosity as by economic gain, who toil away into the quiet hours of the night. They spend time assembling, testing, rethinking, and occasionally scorching the electrical equipment they hope to perfect.

These men are employees of the Westinghouse Electric and Manufacturing Company. The experiments they conduct are both their work, and, strangely, their recreation. There is a gee-whiz quality to the things they do, and they love to do it all.

The interior of the building is a maze of metal, machines, and wire. Inside the largest room, at the center of the building, four men are gathered to conduct an unofficial after-hours experiment. One of them stands at the far end of the room, looking small and lost under the sixty-foot-high ceiling. Beside him is a tall metal cylinder topped by a five-foot-tall wire cage. He crouches low, adjusting a bolt on the floor, grumbling to himself in a heavy Eastern European accent. His voice remains unheard by the others because of the tremendous noise filling the room.

At the other end of the space, two men tend to a pair of carriage-size generators, which whir and screech like out-of-control trolley cars. In the background, barely noticeable, is the hiss and clank of a kerosene-fed steam engine that drives the generators.

A fourth man stands on a platform above them all. He adjusts the wooden tripod under his camera and plays with the focus.

The man near the cylinder stands up, finally satisfied that the bolts are tight. He shouts something across the room. Heads shake. They can't hear him. One of the men, his gray mechanic's coat flapping, jogs the length of the room. "What did you say, Nikola?"

"I said get ready to throw the switch!" Nikola shouts back.

"So it's time?"

"Yes, it's time."

"But you need to stand clear! Get away from there!"

"Nonsense, the electrical field will reach out and up. That's how it's designed. It won't come down at me."

"I don't think that's right. It's dangerous to stand there!"

"Look, I know how the sparks will jump. Trust me. They will arc right over to that other ball." He points to a two-foot orb mounted on a side wall. "They will not reach down here." He looks back at the base cylinder.

"Bahhh … wait a moment. The bottom part of the cage is still not properly aligned. Get the ladder."

Ladder in place, Nikola climbs up several feet, tugging at the cage, hitting it a bit with his hand. Then he climbs down and adjusts the base bolts again until he's satisfied that everything is straight.

"This is aggravating," he laments. "We make do with whatever we can borrow. Working at night. This should be our greatest work, and it's the poor stepchild to Westinghouse!"

"I'm still not sure I understand," says the technician. "We already know you can make lightning. What will it prove?"

"It's not just about lightning, Hans! It's about understanding the energy. I've told you that. It's about waves. Studying them. Studying how they travel, through the sky. Through the earth. There's something here that I'm only beginning to understand. Experiments, son! That's how we understand the mysteries of the universe. We experiment and we look and we see for ourselves." His eyes look wide and wild as he states his case.

Hans takes the ladder away, and Nikola stands, hands on his hips.

The other technician, Raymond, wanders over. "Does this experiment have anything to do with the radio waves you've mentioned? Using them to talk?"

"I don't know yet. It might. I hope that it will help us with that."

"But this doesn't look like a radio experiment."

"It's all connected. More than you realize."

Raymond looks up at the silver ball. "How will you know?"

"For now, we just look at the waves we create. We look at how the electrical fields react. We measure what we find on this small scale, and we expand from there."

Both Hans and Raymond laugh. *Small scale?*

"But Nikola! This is the largest thing we've ever built. It's incredible!"

Nikola waves them off as if they're pesky flies. "Go to your stations now! Get ready!"


The ever-expanding experiments of Nikola Tesla is what keeps these men employed. About half his work week is directly related to Westinghouse products and technology development. The rest of the time is for him alone. The time that he spends with his experiments is both his passion and his obsession. He's not an easy man to work for, yet this wild-eyed engineer builds things that are remarkable enough that other engineers are pulled into his orbit. They stay late and they help where they can. They're not here for the money. They're here for the wonder of it all.

Hans is one of the young engineers who lingers and learns. But he's troubled by this latest experiment. It's so grand and difficult to manage that it seems to cross some sort of line.

"I don't know, sir," he says as he looks at Nikola standing beneath the structure. "We're not supposed to be doing this. None of this is authorized."

"Hans, Hans, Hans," Tesla lectures the twenty-five-year-old. "George Westinghouse is making hundreds of thousands of dollars, maybe millions of dollars, off my patents. And I'm producing more for him every day. If I want to do some experiments using his equipment, I'm damn well going to do them. We'll break things now and then, to be sure. But eventually we'll make him even more money."

He sees the engineer's nervousness. "You don't have to be here. But you wanted to come see it and you wanted to help."

"Yes. But—"

"No *buts!*" His thick dark mustache curls around his upper lip as he shouts. "I'm sure Raymond will throw the switch if you don't."

He waves at Raymond who shrugs, unsure in all the noise if he's being asked to do something.

"No, that's okay. I'll do it. I want to do it."

"All right. Go over there and throw the damn switch then and let me worry about the rest!" He turns and waves to the camera man, who bends and thrusts his head under a dark cloth hanging from the back of bulky wooden box.

Nikola steps back and squats on the floor, looking up at the support structure and the cage. A set of sensors and dials sits in front of him on the floor. He's going to watch the whole thing from right there, crouching beneath the electrical field.

Hans balls his hands into fists as he walks to the generator. A table in front of the machinery holds a makeshift switch, a brass lever about one foot long. There's also a short wall separating the table from the rest of the room. He feels like he's in a bunker, but the walls are not quite protective enough.

Wires run from the generator to the switch, and from the switch a set of longer, heavier wires run down the center of the room toward the tall column.

Raymond runs to the farthest edge of the room, into a doorway. Peeks around the corner.

Hans nods to Tesla and cranks the generator up to full power. He lets it idle for two minutes then pushes the big lever down by its insolated handle. When it reaches the contact points, there is a crackle and a loud hum. At the far end of the room, the pillar inside the cage also starts to hum. In a few seconds a bluish-yellow glow begins to build around the cage. After fifteen seconds the electrical field becomes visible at the top of the cage, a blue arc dancing along the edge with a loud buzz and crackle. Suddenly a jagged finger of light reaches toward the orb. As it makes contact, an arc the size of a lightning bolt forms between the two, humming and crackling across the room. Nikola looks up, pointing to the photographer, who clicks away, quickly sliding big glass negatives in and out of the back of his camera.

The bitter scent of ozone fills the air.

Nikola shouts something that's lost in the noise. He finally motions for the photographer to move down the platform. He does so, nervously dragging his equipment forward. Raymond steps out of his hiding place and starts tending the machines, oiling the spinning hubs of both generators. The hum changes slightly and both dynamos start to spin a bit faster. The glow at the top of the cylinder brightens. Suddenly, a second bright arc reaches out from the top of the structure.

The photographer steps back, rubbing his hand on the back of his neck. He then grabs the top of his head, and his hair seems to be rising. The arc reaches directly toward him with a loud snap. It curves down toward the platform, then lashes sideways like a whip, striking both the camera and the photographer. Both are slapped backwards about ten feet. The man lands hard on his back and lies motionless. The camera clatters to the floor.

Tesla motions for Hans to cut the power. The young man lifts the switch, and the noise and the electric arcs immediately stop. Raymond climbs up a ladder while Tesla continues to squat low, waiting for the electric charge in the air to dissipate.

When Raymond reaches the photographer, he finds the man groaning and rocking side to side, holding his head. His hair is singed, and there's a scorch mark on his face and another on the front of the battered camera. Its wooden frame is broken, either from the shock or the fall, and the negatives are cracked and splayed on the floor.

The other two men finally rush up the ladder.

"Is he okay?"

"Well, he's alive."

Hans and Raymond help the photographer to his feet, but Nikola rushes to the broken negatives instead. Staring at them. "Blast! They're ruined! Now we have no record."

The photographer coughs and rubs his temples. Catching his breath, he looks at the mess, then at Tesla. "Yeah. I'm fine. Thanks for asking." The sarcasm makes Raymond chuckle, but it's lost on Tesla.

Hans pulls the camera upright and looks at the lens. "At least this part's not cracked. Shutter still works."

"God damn it!" the photographer sneers. "I didn't know it would do that! Why didn't anyone tell me? I might have been killed!"

"Nonsense."

"Like hell it's nonsense. You're a dangerous group of men. I don't think I'll be doing business with you again." He gathers his equipment and slowly climbs down. Once on the floor he quickly heads for the door.

"There will be trouble if he reports this," Hans whispers. "We're not supposed to be risking these generators like this."

"Bah," Tesla says again. "What is Westinghouse going to do? Fire me? I think not." His eyes scan the room. "But I do need a larger place than this. And I need someplace far away from here, where anxious eyes won't watch what we do."

His hand rubs his chin. "Someplace where I can build a larger lab. Bigger orbs. Someplace with my own special funding where I don't have to borrow and steal equipment."

As they take down the cables and clean up, Hans chides, "You must have the money by now to build your own place.

You have more patents than anyone I know. Westinghouse is killing Edison because of you."

Tesla smiles. "Indeed." He tosses the negatives in a trash bin, swearing under his breath. "And soon enough, I will make the move. But for now, our research is centered right here."

He looks at the men, first one, and then the other.

"I'm glad you think I'm wealthy. But much of what I earn here goes right back into buying what I need to keep the experiments going. I buy the things that I need. Things that Mr. Westinghouse won't supply." He motions to the cylinder and the orb. "Like these things right here, which you'd better take apart and get them stored."

As they dismantle the experiment, Hans asks about the test. "Did you pick up anything during the sparks? Any radio waves?"

"Not that I could see. But the experiment didn't run long enough."

"Isn't a bigger spark supposed to produce bigger waves?"

"That's one of the things I'm testing, but no, I'm starting to think it doesn't work quite that way. Making the waves stronger isn't just a matter of making bigger sparks."

"Well, if this radio, or radio waves, or whatever, can really do what you say, I think you could end up being the wealthiest man in the country."

Tesla smiles. "You think so? Well, that means we need to beat men like Marconi, and some of the other clowns who are trying to do the same thing. And it means we need funding—lots of it—and I don't think I'm going to get that here. Old George just wants to sell more power to old ladies who want to read their newspapers in the evening."

He looks over to his workbench. "I thought I had an investor lined up. A very wealthy diamond merchant in England. We were supposed to show him a little prototype a colleague of mine built for him. But I'm not sure now that's going to happen."

"Why not?" Raymond asks.

Tesla shrugs. "Let's just say there was a change in the weather. So we'll just have to build another one and try again. Now let's get this stuff away so the morning crew doesn't see it."

# Chapter 22

## *Northwest*

Eventually Amanda rises, hastily preparing for her nighttime departure. As she dresses, she can hear a steady hiss coming from the barn. Elmer, God bless him, has stayed awake and started the engine of the steam wagon. He's a wonderful, silly man, and she wonders why he doesn't just go to bed to get his rest. He deserves it.

She finishes dressing and starts to pack her bag when she hears a sharp knock on the front door of the Quincys' farmhouse. Amanda and Agnes Quincy both step out into the hall. They nervously catch each other's gaze but remain silent. Agnes, white hair awry, is in her nightclothes, clutching the white cotton gown tightly around her neck.

Amanda wonders if it's Wayne but doesn't voice her concern. It's certainly possible that he's tracked her down to this hiding place. If he asked enough people, one of them was bound to know where he could find a white-haired woman who doesn't mind driving a wagon. Especially a woman who's recently allowed a younger woman to come live in her home.

Suddenly Elmer isn't in the barn anymore. He's back inside, and they can hear him hastily lighting a fire in the kitchen stove. He places a kettle on the front burner, hoping it will start hissing—to mask the steamy hiss emanating from behind the house. Elmer walks through the front hall and answers the door just as the visitor knocks again.

"Elmer Quincy?"

"What? Well, of course I am, Tucker. You know it's me."

Upstairs Agnes covers her mouth. She rushes to Amanda's side and whispers, "Tucker is the town constable. Oh my …."

Downstairs, Tucker continues. "Listen, Elmer, I feel funny about this, but I need to do my official duty. You understand? That's the only reason I'm asking you officially what your name is. Of course I know who you are. My father's known you for years."

Elmer is very cordial as he invites the young constable inside.

"Listen, I'm sorry to bother you, Elmer. Especially at this hour. I know it has to be after midnight. I thought you'd be in bed, what with you being sick and all!"

Elmer fights the urge to look toward the stairs. "Well, usually I am. But I had some extra chores this evening. Now I'm fixing a cup of tea. Do you want one?"

"Oh no. All right, then. Here's the official business that brings me here. Some fool farmer over by the Brewster line says his wife ran out on him. And he says your wife helped his wife come back and steal some of his belongings. Says she stabbed him too."

Upstairs, Agnes looks at Amanda.

"I didn't," Amanda whispers. "He swung at me. I told you I just blocked… "

Agnes shushes her. "It's okay. We just need to get you out to the barn."

There is no back stairway in the house. The front stairs would take them right past where the men are standing.

"How do we get out?"

She motions to Amanda to follow her into a back bedroom. Below them the conversation continues, with Elmer trying to stall for time.

"Is your wife around?" the constable asks.

"Yes, but she's sleeping, Tucker."

"Well, I guess I won't ask you to wake her just yet. But what about that woman? Do you have the woman here?"

"Well, I ... I did ...." His voice is just loud enough so that it drifts upstairs, meant as a warning to the women.

Agnes nods. "Good. He didn't exactly lie. He won't get in trouble for lying at least."

"What do you mean you did?" Tucker demands.

"Well, I mean she was here for a while. But she left. I mean. I think she did."

"Dad-burn it, Elmer, you *think* she did? You mean you don't know?"

Agnes pushes Amanda ahead of her. They tiptoe to the window, which, thankfully, is already open on this warm night. Amanda manages to wiggle through it and out onto a porch roof.

"Can you reach the tree?" Agnes asks in a loud whisper as she leans out the window.

Amanda tries. "No. It's too far!" She looks down and sees that the ground slopes sharply away from the porch. It's not a safe distance to jump.

"Try the downspout!"

Amanda walks to the corner of the roof and tugs at it. Notched into the wooden gutter, the downspout is an iron pipe, painted white. It seems solid enough, so she nods.

Agnes slides Amanda's bag out the window. "Drop that down first. I'll meet you out by the barn." She disappears back into the bedroom.

Amanda listens to the hiss of the steam engine. Every few moments the engine thuds slightly. She waits for the next thud and drops the bag so the sound of its landing is covered by the noise.

Gripping the downspout, she closes her eyes, shivers, then swings over, all her weight hanging by her hands. She can't hug the pipe like a fireman's pole because it's too tight against the house. The best she can do is to quickly lower herself, hand over hand, hurrying before her strength gives out. Her hands make a squeaking sound and her shoes clunk a bit. As Amanda slides past the lower window, she hears the constable ask about the noise coming from the barn.

"Oh, that?" Elmer laughs, "It's that blasted steam engine. You know, the one that I have. It's been leaking like a sieve. I patched it today. Just wanted to test it. Fired it up a while ago."

"In the middle of the night?"

"Oh, I'm letting it idle overnight with the valve half open. Needs a good long test. If there's any water under the boiler in the morning, then I'll know it's still leaking."

"Jesus, Elmer, you've left that thing fired up and running all alone out in the barn? That doesn't seem safe!"

Amanda reaches the ground and collects her bag. She hears Agnes enter the room and walk across it to face the constable. "No, it's not safe, is it? Hello Tucker. Good to see you again. How's your father?"

"Yes, hi ma'am. Good … good thanks."

"You know I tried to tell him that it wasn't safe. He just won't listen."

"Agnes, please," Elmer tries to interrupt with fake exasperation.

"I did! I said it wasn't safe, didn't I? And when I couldn't talk you out of doing that silly test, I said to at least move it out of the barn. But no … had to do it where you wanted to do it."

They argue for over two minutes, with the constable looking back and forth between them, flustered and trying to get a word in.

Outside, Amanda realizes this is the diversion she needs, and she runs toward the barn.

In the front hallway the constable finally places a hand between the husband and wife, separating them. "Mr. and Mrs. Quincy! Please! Can we just get back to the question? Is that woman here or not?"

Elmer coughs a raspy cough. "I said I'm not sure!"

Agnes takes the constable aside. "You know Elmer's not well. He forgets things. I don't think his judgment is the best right now."

"Then why don't you answer for him! I asked is that woman here?"

"Oh. Well, yes, I guess I could." She realizes she's nearly out of time. "She is upstairs. I guess I could go wake her up."

"Please do. She has a lot of explaining to do."

"I really didn't realize all we were getting into with her ...." She catches Elmer's eye and tilts her head toward the kitchen before going upstairs.

"How did you get involved in this, Elmer?" the constable asks.

"Well, don't rightly know. I don't think she's a bad woman though, Tucker. I don't think that at all. It's her husband who's the bad one, from what I can see."

"Well, we need to let the law decide that. You know that very well, Mr. Quincy."

Agnes waits several moments, then calls to the constable to follow her upstairs. As soon as he climbs up, Elmer limps to the kitchen and picks up a sack before slipping out the back door.

"Agnes made you a bag of sandwiches," he tells Amanda, who is already sitting in the driver's seat, studying the levers and trying to remember the previous day's driving lesson. "And your silverware is in here too. You need to get out of here fast, dear. And I mean fast!" After a quick hug and words of encouragement, he shoves open the barn door.

"I'll miss this old contraption," Elmer shouts. "You take care of it, you hear?"

"Thank you, sir," Amanda smiles at him. "I do appreciate your generosity."

"Oh, I almost forgot. Here. You'll need these." Elmer hands her a set of thick goggles, leather at the edges and with cloudy glass in the center. One lens is slightly cracked.

"The old wind whips up pretty good when you're on the straightaways. These old goggles are the only thing I have to block it."

She takes them and puts them on, then pushes them back onto the top of her head. She nods toward the puzzle box, which sits on the floor beside her. "Say, if I get stuck trying to open the rest of this box, do you remember where that antique dealer is? The one you said collects and sells them?"

Elmer thinks for a moment. "Somewhere near the edge of Beacon Hill. The first street at the foot of the hill where a group of shops can be found. I can't say exactly where. Chinaman runs it. Now get moving!"

She leans back against a tall bench that Elmer had nailed in place behind the steering levers. She feels like she's captaining a ship. The wagon hisses as Amanda pulls the big lever. It jerks too quickly as she releases the clutch. The mistake shoots her out into the yard and scares the constable's horse. It runs off into the Quincys' side field.

Amanda grips the steering levers with white knuckles and manages to weave her way across the lawn, much faster than she intended. The wagon slides sideways as she turns onto the road. She overcorrects and feels the rear platform waving like the tail of a horse. *Stay calm. Remember the lessons.* Lip pinched tightly between her teeth.

Pulling slightly on one lever and pushing hard on another, she fights to realign the clattering cart. Eventually it straightens and she's able to accelerate up the road.

Behind her the screen door slams, and the constable runs out into the yard. "What the hell was that?"

"Blasted girl slipped out of her room and came down here! She stole my damn wagon!"

Agnes joins them in the darkness beneath the trees. The constable squints at them both suspiciously. When he turns to look for his horse he realizes it's run away.

"God damn it! All right, Elmer. Look here. Our families have known each other for a long time, so I'm going to let this one slide. I shouldn't, but I know you're sick, and frankly I don't much care for the man who filed this complaint. But the only way I'm going to ignore what happened tonight is if you loan me one of your damn horses so I can get back to town!"

"Certainly, certainly. I've got one right over here." He steers the constable toward Duncan, neglecting to mention that the horse has a lame hoof.

A mile or so down the road Amanda's heart still races. The wind draws tears from her eyes, and she remembers the goggles. Pulling them down, she feels like a small bug perched atop a swooping dragonfly. *Deep breath.*

She steps through the sequence that allows her to ramp up the steam wagon's gears. The ever-thoughtful Elmer has tied a lantern to the front of the water tank. Its circle of light extends only about twenty-five feet. Luckily there is half a moon. Eyes now adjusted to the dim light, she can see the road fairly well. After a mile or two, she smiles a slight smile and tosses a few more lumps of coal onto the fire.

"Good wagon," she finds herself saying, treating it like she might treat a horse. She pats the top of the seat. "Let's get us there, okay?"

Small dots of hot orange trail back from the top of the smoke stack. A bump in the road prompts a small hiss from the tank as the water sloshes side to side.

She adjusts the gears again, preparing to slow the rig as she approaches a curve. "I don't know where we're heading exactly, wagon, but you need to get us there. I'll take care of you if you take care of me. Is that a deal?"

Wind against the goggles. Cool night air against her cheeks. Coming out of the curve, she clicks a couple notches back up on the speed lever. West toward Sandwich and Sagamore. Then northwest through Plymouth and beyond.

She roars on into the night, hissing and clanking and smoking. Amanda heads back toward the glow of the big city, with sparks trailing behind her like dying moths.

The Puzzle Box Chronicles is a series, starting with
Book 1 –Wreck of the Gossamer

\* \* \* \*

The Story of Amanda, Jeb, Wayne, Victor, Devlin and others
continues in

**The Lost, the Found and the Hidden**
The Puzzle Box Chronicles: Book 2

**Those Who Wander**
The Puzzle Box Chronicles: Book 3

**Wires and Wings**
The Puzzle Box Chronicles: Book 4

**North of Angel Falls**
The Puzzle Box Chronicles: Book 5

**The Beckoning Spark**
The Puzzle Box Chronicles: Book 6

---

## Did you enjoy this book?
### *Online reviews are always appreciated!*

Small press publishers rely on readers to help spotlight
interesting authors and stories.

**Thank you!**

---

Made in the USA
Monee, IL
26 June 2023

37602450R00115